TERROR STALKS
TRAVERSE CITY

Look for more 'Michigan Chillers' including:

#1: Mayhem on Mackinac Island
#2: Terror Stalks Traverse City
#3: Poltergeists of Petoskey
#4: Aliens Attack Alpena
#5: Gargoyles of Gaylord
#6: Strange Spirits of St. Ignace
#7: Kreepy Klowns of Kalamazoo
#8: Dinosaurs Destroy Detroit
#9: Sinister Spiders of Saginaw
#10: Mackinaw City Mummies

and
'American Chillers'
including:

#1: The Michigan Mega-Monsters
#2: Ogres of Ohio
#3: Florida Fog Phantoms
#4: New York Ninjas
#5: Terrible Tractors of Texas
#6: Invisible Iguanas of Illinois
#7: Wisconsin Werewolves
#8: Minnesota Mall Mannequins
#9: Iron Insects Invade Indiana

AudioCraft Publishing, Inc.
PO Box 281
Topinabee Island, MI 49791

#2: Terror Stalks Traverse City

JOHNATHAN
RAND

An AudioCraft Publishing, Inc. book

Graphics layout/design consultant: Chuck Beard, Straits Area Printing, Cheboygan, MI

ISBN 1-893699-07-2

Printed in USA

Sixth printing, April 2003

Visit the official 'Chillers' web site at:

www.americanchillers.com

Featuring excerpts from upcoming stories, interviews, and
MORE!

Terror Stalks Traverse City

Ever since I can remember, I've always wanted to be a magician. You know the kind . . . like the ones you see on TV that can make animals disappear and saw people in half. Well, not *really* saw them in half, but they sure make it look like they do! Once on TV, I saw a magician make a whole plane disappear. I know it was only a trick, but it sure was cool.

But last Christmas one of my presents was a magic kit . . . and let me tell you, it changed my mind completely about wanting to be a magician!

The problem started a couple days before Christmas. I was upstairs in my bedroom, and my sister was downstairs watching TV.

"Matt!" my dad hollered up to me. "A package came for you in the mail today! You too, Kimmy!"

A package? For me? And Kimmy? Cool! I hardly ever get mail!

"Ohboyohboyohboy!" I heard my sister shout from downstairs. She's six years old and gets excited about anything. I'm eleven, so I've been around the block a few more times than her.

But I was still excited to get something in the mail!

I ran downstairs to find two large, brown packages on the kitchen table. Kimmy was already there, her eyes all bugged out at the sight of a box waiting for her and her alone.

"I think they're from Grandma and Grandpa," Dad said.

I picked up the package and read the address label.

Mr. Matthew Sorenson
2456 Willow Street
Traverse City, MI 49685

But right below the label was a note that got me really excited:

Do NOT wait till Christmas! Open immediately!

Cool!

"Can I open mine, Daddy?" Kimmy asked.

"Well, the note says not to wait," Dad said. "So I guess you'd better open it right away."

I didn't even ask Dad if I could open mine! I knew already that I was supposed to open it.

I couldn't wait. Grandma and Grandpa always get me the coolest stuff. Last year Grandpa got me a model rocket that really worked! This year . . . well, who knows?

I cut the packaging tape with a pair of scissors and opened the box. Inside was a card addressed to me, and a bunch of popcorn. You know the kind of popcorn I'm talking about ... those little white puffy kernels made of foam. They keep whatever is inside the box from shifting around and getting damaged.

I shuffled through the popcorn with my hands and found still another package. This one was wrapped in blue and gold Christmas wrapping paper. A silver bow was attached to the top of it.

Kimmy had already opened up her package and was tearing off the wrapping paper on her gift. She had spilled white foam popcorn all over the floor.

"It's a Barbie!" she suddenly yelled.

"Do you have to be so loud?" I said. Kimmy has this really high-pitched voice. She can be so annoying sometimes. She just stuck out her tongue at me.

Typical sister.

I began tearing into the wrapping paper. What was it going to be this year? A model airplane? Maybe a super giant ant farm! That would be neat!

But when I tore away the final layer of wrapping paper, I just stared.

"Wow," I whispered.

I couldn't believe what I was seeing.

I read the big block letters out loud:

"**PROFESSIONAL STAGE MAGICIAN KIT**," it read. Right beneath that: *"Over 100 magic tricks included!"*

"Wow!" I said again, only this time I didn't whisper. A magic kit! I had always wanted one! How did Grandma and Grandpa know?

"Lemmee see! Lemmee see!" Kimmy shouted.

"Go on, go play with your doll," I said, turning away from her. For once, she listened to me. She picked up her Barbie and went into the living room.

I looked at the box, reading the words again.

This was going to be fun!

My own magic kit.   Card tricks, disappearing tricks . . . it was all there.

My very own magic kit.

I couldn't wait. I had to go learn some magic right away. Then I could show everyone some magic tricks for Christmas! Uncle Dave and Aunt Kate would be coming, and of course my twin cousins, Alex and Adrian. Maybe I could even put on a magic show!

But I'd have to get started. Christmas was only three days away. That didn't give me much time to learn a lot of magic tricks.

I took the box upstairs to my room and opened it up. I spread out the contents all over my bed. There was a manual, a hat, a cape, and all kinds of cool stuff.

This was going to be a great Christmas! The best ever.

Now, looking back, I wish I'd NEVER opened up that box. I didn't know it at the time,

but what was about to happen almost wrecked
Christmas — not only for me, but for everybody
in Traverse City!

Maybe I could have prevented any problems if I would have read the manual first. But I was in such a hurry to get started that I began playing around with the things that were included in the magic kit. I never even gave the manual a second glance.

Not yet, anyway.

I shuffled through a deck of trick cards. I found a small plastic tube that was supposed to make a penny disappear. There was also a small box that had a secret opening in the bottom to make it look like whatever was placed in the box would vanish.

Then I found the magic wand.

It looked just like you would expect a magic wand to look like. It was about as long as my arm and all black, except for a white tip. Very cool.

Just then I heard banging on my door.

"Matt!" I heard Kimmy say. "Matt! I wanna see your magic kit!"

"Go away," I said. "I'm learning how to do magic."

"But I wanna see!" she persisted. Sometimes she can be such a pest.

"All right," I said. "But when I open up this door I'm going to make you disappear."

That did the trick. I heard her footsteps running away from the door and back downstairs.

"Dad!" I heard her shout. "Daddy . . . Matt is going to make me disappear! Don't let him, Daddy!"

Sisters.

I experimented with the cards for a few

minutes. It looked like an ordinary deck, except there were a couple special cards. There was even a trick card that shot water like a water pistol! That would be fun.

There was also a small tray that turned a one-dollar bill into a five-dollar bill. That would be even MORE fun!

And a black hat. It was a real magician's hat, one that you wore on your head and pulled rabbits out of.

Well, I guess I kind of figured you could pull rabbits out of it. There certainly weren't any rabbits included with the kit.

I plopped the hat on my head and looked into the mirror.

"Hey," I said to myself. "That looks good." I really *did* look like a magician. My black hair stuck out from the sides of the hat. I'm taller than most kids my age, and a little thinner, too. The hat made me look even taller. I think I might have looked like a young Abraham Lincoln, except he had a really big nose. I don't.

I rummaged through the stuff on my bed

and found another part of the magician's uniform . . . a long black cape.

I draped it over my shoulders and looked into the mirror again.

That looked even better. Wow! Was this going to be a cool Christmas! I was going to do magic tricks for everyone on Christmas day.

But my outfit wasn't complete yet. All I needed to really look like a magician was—

The magic wand.

I picked it up and looked into the mirror.

"That's cool," I whispered. I really *did* look like a magician.

I held the wand up, and waved it back and forth, pretending to make something disappear. I thought it would be really fun if I could make something vanish.

Little did I know I was about to make something *really* disappear.

And that's when the trouble began.

On my wall I have a paper drawing that I made in school. It was a drawing of lots of Christmas things—a snowman, a bunch of elves, Santa's reindeer, and a snow monster. The snow monster looked creepy. I gave him big red eyes and long fangs and white hair all over his body. The elves were all different colors and had pointed hats with a little dingle-ball on top. Their chins were pointy and so were their noses.

I decided that I would make the poster disappear.

"Aleekazaam!" I shouted as I waved the wand in the air. As I spoke, I pointed the wand at the poster.

The poster stayed right where it was, taped to the wall.

Hmmm. That didn't work. I wondered what else I could try.

I looked around the room, and something outside my window caught my attention. I walked over to the window and peered down at the snow-covered yard below.

It was getting dark, but there was still enough light to see pretty well.

And what I saw made my eyes go wide and my jaw drop.

There were tiny elves running all over the yard! And reindeer! Even a snowman was walking around!

I rubbed my eyes, not believing what I was seeing.

But it was real! I could see them as clear as anything.

That's when I suddenly realized something, and I turned around in shock, afraid of what I would see.

The poster.

The paper was still on the wall, but all of my drawings—the elves, the reindeer, the snowman— all of them were missing! They were no longer on the paper!

I turned around again and looked down into the yard.

The elves were running about all over the place, and the reindeer were, too. They had even gone into our neighbor's yard . . . and boy, had they started to cause problems! The elves were climbing up trees that had been decorated. They were pulling off the lights and throwing them into the snow. I could see them smiling and laughing at their own mischievousness.

"Hey!" I yelled at them through the window. "Hey! You can't do that!"

I didn't think that they could hear me, but one of the elves that had climbed up a Christmas tree looked up.

He stuck his tongue out at me!

This was not good. This was not good at all.

The reindeer had gotten into my mom's flower garden. Obviously there were no flowers, just snow — but the reindeer pawed at the ground and dug up dirt! They left big holes in the garden! Mom's gonna freak!

I still couldn't believe what I was seeing. The creatures in my drawing had actually come to life. They were scurrying about all over the yard and into the street.

Suddenly, one of the elves climbed the light post in front of our house. The post was decorated with lights and tinsel and garland.

Do you know what that little stinker did? He pulled everything off! And I mean everything! He yanked off the colorful Christmas lights and they all blinked out. He pulled down the tinsel and garland, slid down the post, and stomped all over the decorations! It was crazy! They were going to destroy the whole yard!

Suddenly I shivered, and I turned and looked back at the blank poster on the wall.

If the elves had come alive . . . .

And the reindeer were alive, too . . . .

And if the snowman had come alive . . . .
Then that would mean . . . .
I shuddered at the thought.
The snow monster.
He was alive, too!

I don't think I have ever felt more scared in my life. Ever. Well, okay — maybe once. Last year I watched a really scary movie on TV. I had nightmares for weeks!

But that was just a movie. This was *real*. This was actually happening, and I was the one who started it all!

What was I going to do? I mean . . . I couldn't just watch while the elves and reindeer and the snowman demolished the front yard.

But even worse . . . what had become of

the snow monster? Again, I looked at my poster, hoping that somehow this was all some huge mistake. I hoped that if I looked again, the snowman and the reindeer and the elves . . . and the *snow monster* . . . would be on the paper.

No luck. The white sheet just stared back at me from the wall.

I looked down into the yard again. Tiny sprinkles of snow had started to fall, and most of the elves had run across the street.

Now they were wrecking another yard! They had finished their destruction in our yard, and were moving on to find more things to wreck. They were going to destroy the whole neighborhood!

I looked down the street, and in the growing darkness I saw a horrifying sight.

It was big. And it was *ugly*.

The snow monster.

He was standing on the hood of a car, jumping up and down, pounding his chest like Tarzan. His white hair shook with every leap, and with every pounce, a dent would form on the car hood.

And he was *huge.* He was easily twice the size of a grownup.

Now what would I do?

Suddenly I had an idea. If I had waved the wand at the poster and my drawing had come to life, maybe if I waved my wand at the creatures they would go back to the poster! It was worth a shot.

Of course, anything was worth a shot at this point!

I snapped up the black magic wand and pointed it at one of the elves on the other side of the street. He was sitting in a Christmas tree, throwing bulbs onto the ground, laughing hysterically as the bulbs exploded into a million tiny pieces.

"Aleekazaam!" I said.

All of a sudden the elf stopped and looked right at me! Somehow, he must've heard me.

Was it going to work?

I turned and looked back at the poster.

No elf.

But when I turned back around, there were suddenly *two* elves in the tree! I had created another one with my magic wand!

I am in a *lot* of trouble.

The magic kit was still on my bed. I ran to it and picked up the manual, then ran back to the window. Standing in front of the pane I could keep an eye on the strange scene below and flip through the manual. Maybe there was something in there that could help.

On page one, my heart sank. I felt a lump grow in my throat. In big bold letters, a warning on the page said:

CAUTION—NEVER USE MAGIC WAND WHILE WEARING CAPE *AND* HAT!

I spun and looked in the mirror.

I was still wearing the cape and hat! If only I had read the manual first!

I threw the hat to the ground and pulled the cape off.

What next? I couldn't just stand by and let the whole neighborhood be destroyed. Mom and Dad would be furious.

Or worse.

I flipped frantically through the manual. Finally, near the back, there was a troubleshooting guide. As I read, my heart sank again.

To return anything to its former condition, simply touch it with the white tip of the magic wand. *WARNING: It MUST be touched with the WHITE TIP to completely reverse the magic.*

Huh?

In other words, to get the elves back onto my poster, I'd have to touch each one with the wand?

That's crazy!

I mean . . . that might be fine for the elves and the reindeer and the snowman—but what about the snow monster? I didn't even want to get *close* to him! He would tear me limb from limb!

I stood there, wondering what to do, when I heard an enormous crash from outside. The noise surprised me and I jumped. I looked

31

out the window.

    Oh no!

6

The elves had banded together and toppled the Christmas tree across the street! They were jumping up and down in victory, tossing bulbs into the snow, laughing in devilish delight. One of the elves ran along the branch of the Christmas tree and raised his arms in victory while the other elves cheered him on. A reindeer was eating one of the branches.

This was a nightmare!

And the only way to stop them would be to touch each and every one of them with my magic wand.

I was going to need some help. There was no way I could do this alone.

I stuffed the wand into my back pocket, sprang out of my bedroom, and ran downstairs. Mom caught me as I reached the living room.

"Young man," she began. (Whenever I'm getting scolded she calls me 'young man'.) "Young man, how many times have I told you not to run down the stairs?"

"Whoops. Sorry Mom. I forgot. I'm going to go outside for a few minutes, okay?"

Mom looked out the window. "Okay," she said. "But not for long. Tomorrow is a school day."

We have a phone downstairs in the basement and I snuck down there to use it.

I decided to call John Miller. He lives down the street, and we've been friends forever. I could trust him.

The phone rang and rang.

Come on, I thought. *Answer the phone, John. Answer the phone.*

Suddenly, I heard a click on the other end

of the phone.

"Hello?" It was John's mom.

"Hi Mrs. Miller," I began. "This is Matt Sorenson. Is John there?"

"Yes, he is, but he's outside right now cleaning up."

Outside cleaning up? What did she mean by that? Cleaning up *what?*

"I beg your pardon, Mrs. Miller?"

"Yes, he's outside cleaning up. Some vandals came by and pulled all of the lights from our tree outside. They made an awful mess."

Whoops. *Giant* whoops.

"Uh . . . okay," I said. "I'll run down and help out."

"Oh, that's so nice of you," she said. "Whoever is responsible, they've sure made a mess of things around here."

I hung up the phone.

Yeah, I thought. *That's so nice of me. Wait till everyone finds out I'm responsible for this whole thing.*

I ran back upstairs and put on my

snowsuit. I was careful to put the magic wand in the pocket of my snowsuit, too. And just to be on the safe side, I stuffed the magician's manual into my inside pocket.

"Don't forget a hat," Mom hollered from the living room.

Moms.

The air outside was cold and crisp. Thick snow whirled about in the air, blown by a light wind. I like winter, and the cold doesn't bother me at all. What bothered me right now was the mess that the elves and reindeer had left behind.

The yards were a mess! When people came out of their houses and found all of their Christmas decorations in shambles, they would be madder than a swarm of hornets!

I ran down the street, my heart racing. My snow boots squawked on the hard-packed snow as I thundered past houses and parked cars. Everywhere I looked, I saw destruction. Broken Christmas lights, broken bulbs, Christmas trees that had been knocked down—it was *terrible!*

I ran faster, my legs pumping in the

newly-fallen dusting of snow. Soon, I was at John's house.

He was outside, just like his mom had said. Christmas lights had been yanked from the eves of their home, and John was winding up the string around his arm.

"John!" I shouted from the street. He turned and waved.

"Hi Matt," he hollered back. "Boy . . . when I get my hands on the kids who did this—"

"Hold on a minute," I said, approaching him. I was out of breath, and I was really huffing and puffing. "I know who did this."

John's eyes grew wide. "What?!?! You do?!?! Who?"

"Elves," I said. "Elves and reindeer and a snowman. And a snow monster."

A scowl came to his face. He scrunched his forehead and furrowed his brow. "Cut the jokes," he said. "This is serious. Somebody is really causing a problem." He wasn't smiling.

"I *am* serious, John. You have to help me. If we don't stop them, I'm afraid they'll destroy half of Traverse City! We need to—"

A sudden shadow caught my attention, and I stopped speaking.

There was something big and white by the corner of John's house.

It was moving fast . . . and it was coming right for us!

7

"Watch out!" I yelled. But it was too late.

The snowman — *my* snowman — was too quick. He smacked right into John, sending him flying! John landed face first in the snow. He stood up immediately, his face wet with snow crystals, his cheeks red with anger.

"All right," he said, turning around. "Somebody's going to —"

He stopped in mid-sentence when he saw the snowman coming at him again.

"What's . . . what's going —"

Boom!

The snowman hit John again, sending him flying into a snow bank. This time John plunged head first into the snow, and I have to admit he looked pretty funny. His whole head was in the snow and all I could see was his arms and legs flailing madly about.

The snowman let out a hearty laugh that boomed over the neighborhood.

"Ohohoho, that was a good one," the snowman bellowed. Not only was he a nasty snowman . . . he was a *talking* nasty snowman!

John popped his head out of the snow and stood up, facing his attacker. He couldn't believe what he was seeing. An honest-to-goodness snowman was alive and running around in his front yard!

"What's going on here, Matt?!?!" John hollered, wiping his face with his gloved hands. I know he didn't believe me before, but he sure did now!

"That's what I was trying to tell you!", I said, throwing up my hands. "That snowman is the one who yanked your lights down. That snowman . . . along with elves and reindeer!" I tried to explain more to him but I had to stop—because now the snowman was headed for *me!*

I ducked sideways and he missed me. It was the craziest thing, watching this snowman with no legs racing about in the yard! He had sticks for arms but he didn't seem to use them. I had drawn him with a stocking cap and a carrot nose, and that is exactly what he had. He just kind of waddled about, swishing quickly through the snow. Everywhere he went, he was followed by a wide path that he cut through the snow.

By now John was back on his feet and by my side.

"This is too weird," he said.

"Yeah, well, there's more," I explained. "That's why you've got to help me."

I pulled out the wand from the pocket of my snowsuit, holding it out before me like a sword.

"Try and draw the snowman's attention," I said. "The manual says I have to touch him to

41

make him go back onto my poster."

"What manual?" John asked. "What poster?" Boy, was he confused. I guess I would be, too, if I were in his shoes.

"I'll explain later," I said quickly. "Right now I've got to get close to him. I've got to touch him with this wand."

The snowman was making another turn in the yard and was now coming back our way.

"Ohohoho, this is fun!" the snowman laughed. He flashed a big smile as he began to charge.

"Call him to you," I told John. "I'll run up behind him and get him with the wand!"

"What?!?! How do you 'call' a snowman?!?!"

But he didn't have to. The snowman was already coming toward him.

I sprang, circling back around behind the snowman as he raced toward John. John tried to run away, but he wasn't fast enough. The snowman was much quicker.

"Matt, I don't know what you're doing, but so help me—"

Boom!

The snowman knocked John to the ground again. He really seemed to be having fun at John's expense.

"Ohohohoho!" the snowman snickered. "Gotcha again! Ohohohoho!"

But his fun was about to be over.

I *hoped*.

I was right behind him when he smacked into John. As he did, I touched the wand to his snowy head.

He stopped instantly, frozen in his tracks.

Poof!

In the next instant he had vanished. No more snowman. There was only a slight popping sound as he disappeared.

John was still laying in the snow, watching. His eyes got huge.

"How did you—"

"That's what I was trying to tell you," I said. "I got a magic kit for Christmas from my Grandma and Grandpa—but it's a *real* magic kit. I accidentally brought to life all of the creatures on my poster."

"Just *what* was on your poster?" he asked, standing up. He brushed the snow from his snowsuit, looking at the place where the snowman had just stood.

"Some elves, some reindeer, a snowman . . . *and a snow monster.*"

John looked at me. "A snow monster?" he said, shuddering.

I nodded my head. "I didn't mean to bring him to life. Honest. But now the elves and the reindeer are destroying the neighborhood. They're going to wreck Christmas for everyone."

"And just what is the snow monster doing?" John asked. His eyes were growing wider by the second. I know he was having a hard time believing all of this.

Just then we heard an unearthly, blood-curdling scream from a few blocks away. It sounded nothing like I have ever heard before in my life. Not a human scream, but a terrifying howl that sent a million shivers down my spine.

Trying to convince John to help me wasn't easy.
Especially after he heard that awful screech in
the night.

"I'm not chasing down any snow monster,
huh-uh, no way, no sir, not gonna happen," he
insisted, shaking his head from side to side with
so much force that I thought it was going to
wobble off.

"You have to," I pleaded. "These things
are going to wreck everyone's Christmas. And
it'll all be my fault. All because I didn't read

that dumb manual."

"Well, where are they now?" he asked, referring to the elves and the reindeer.

"I don't know. Probably running all over Traverse City by now. The elves are small . . . there's seven of them . . . about the size of Rusty." Rusty is our Cocker Spaniel.

"And how big are the reindeer?" he asked.

"A little bit bigger. About the size of a small pony. There's five of them."

He was silent for a moment, then spoke.

"And the snow monster?"

I knew he was going to ask me that.

I didn't want to tell him, but I had to. He had to know the truth. I took a breath and let it out slowly. "Twice the size of your dad," I said somberly.

John's eyes just about popped out of his head. His mouth opened and I thought his jaw was going to fall to the ground. "But," I added, trying to sound more cheerful. "There's only *one* of them."

Suddenly, John's eyes bugged out and his arm shot into the air like a javelin. "There's one right there! An elf!"

I turned to see an elf scurrying up a light post across the street. He had a red vest and a green hat and little blue shoes that curled up at the toes . . . just like I had made him on my poster. He was quick and nimble, too. He climbed the light post as easily as a squirrel could.

"Let's go get him!" I said, immediately taking off running, my boots thumping on the hard-packed snow. "Come on!" John followed, bolting behind me across the street.

The elf was at the top of the light post now, untying strands of garland and yanking at the carefully wound Christmas lights. He was working fast.

"He's wrecking the whole thing," John said.

"Hey you!" I yelled to the elf. "Stop that! Come down here!"

He stuck his tongue out at me! Not only was he an elf . . . but he was a *rude* elf! The worst kind.

"Why, that little bugger!" I said. "I'll

show him!"

I bent over and made a snowball and tossed it up at the elf. I missed by a few inches, and the elf stuck his tongue out at me again!

"Wait!" John said, bending over to make a snowball. "I'll throw the snowball . . . you get your wand ready! That way when he falls, you'll be ready!"

That was a better idea.

John missed with the first snowball, but the second one was right on target. It caught the elf square in the face and sent him flying off the light post!

"Got him!" John shouted triumphantly.

The elf tumbled through the air and fell at our feet. I pounced on him, placing the wand against his shoulder.

He froze instantly, and in the next second —

Poof! He had vanished.

"Way to go!" I said, standing up and giving John a high-five. "One down, six more to go!"

"It doesn't look like we'll get a chance to

get them," John said, raising his arm and pointing. "Take a look."

I looked down the street. My eyes got as big as Garfield's.

A police car was coming toward us!

The police car slowed as it approached. But at least the red and blue lights weren't flashing.

"Now what do we do?" John whispered. "I hope they don't think we're the ones that have been doing all this damage. I don't want to go to jail!"

Neither did I.

The police car stopped in front of us and a uniformed man got out.

"You boys live around here?" he asked.

"Yes sir," John replied. "I live across the

street. Matt lives a few blocks down."

"Well, you both be careful. There's been some strange reports tonight. I'd stay close to home until we know what's going on."

"Okay," we both replied in unison. The policeman got back into his car and drove off.

Whew!

"Strange reports?" I said to John as I watched the police car drive away.

I was beginning to have a really bad feeling about this.

Really bad.

"Come on," I said. "We have to find the snow monster . . .and *fast*. And we have to find the rest of the elves and reindeer before every Christmas decoration in Traverse City has been broken."

"Well, we can get the elves, and maybe the reindeer," John stated. "But what about the snow monster? How do we get him?"

I shook my head. "I don't know," I said. "I guess we'll figure that out when the time comes."

"Well, time's up for a reindeer," John said

excitedly. "There's one right now!"

I turned to see a reindeer standing next to a car at the house next door. He was chewing on the branches of a Christmas tree!

"Oh no!" John whispered loudly. "That's the Wentworth's house! Old man Wentworth is gonna be furious!"

Everybody knew old man Wentworth. He hardly ever came out of his house, and when he did, it was usually to yell at kids that were playing baseball in a nearby yard. He would holler and tell everyone what he would do if a ball so much as even came *close* to his house. Old man Wentworth wasn't a very nice man.

Imagine what he would do if he found a reindeer eating his Christmas tree!

We sprinted across the snow covered yard and slowed as we reached the reindeer. The animal stayed right where it was, chewing on the branches, hardly paying any attention to us. It reminded me of some of the animals I've seen at the petting zoo. Some of them were very timid and shy, and some of them just ignored people altogether.

I pulled out my magic wand and stepped close to the reindeer. Still, the animal hardly paid any attention to us. It just stood there, snow flying about him, eating the tree branch. It was as docile and harmless as a puppy.

I touched the wand to its back and in the next instant it had vanished. Simple as that.

"Well, at least *that* one was easy," I said. "Come on. There's more around."

We walked the entire neighborhood, around and through backyards, and over to the next block. Getting rid of the rest of the reindeer was pretty easy. They were real shy and didn't run away at all. We were able to get all five within a few minutes, along with three more elves.

But they sure made a mess! Everywhere we went, Christmas lights had been pulled down and garland had been strewn about. Some Christmas trees had even been pushed over. Garbage cans had been toppled. It was awful. I was sure it wouldn't be long before people began to notice the damage.

And we were constantly on the lookout

for the snow monster. Once or twice we came across his tracks in the snow. The tracks were huge . . . bigger than anything I had ever seen before. I could put both of my feet inside just one of his prints!

"Let's hope we find him before he finds us," John said.

But what we didn't know was that at that very moment, a pair of unseen eyes were watching our every move.

10

The hands came out of nowhere. We had been sneaking around the corner of a house. John thought he saw an elf dart behind a tree, so we were trying to find it.

Suddenly a pair of hands reached out from the shadows. One grabbed me, the other, John.

"Gotcha, you little trouble makers!" a surly voice hissed. "Thought you could get away with all this, huh? Well, we'll see about *that!*"

It was old man Wentworth!

He spun us around to face him. He was old and kind of creepy looking. And *mad*. He had no hat on, and his white hair tossed about in the night wind. His cheeks were drawn and he had lots of wrinkles on his forehead. I thought we were goners.

"Please sir," I began to explain. "We're not the ones that have been destroying everything. There's some other . . . uh . . . *kids.* They're kids from another neighborhood."

"That's right," John chimed in. "We've been following them. They've been destroying everyone's Christmas decorations. Even *ours.* We're trying to catch them."

The old man looked long and hard into my eyes, then John's, then mine again. He released his grip on our shoulders.

"Oh, sure," he wheezed. His voice was raspy and trembled with anger. "Like I'm supposed to believe *that.* I'm gonna report both of you to—" He stopped in mid-sentence.

"Now . . . what on earth is that?" he said suddenly, looking at something behind us.

I spun and looked at what the old man was looking at. John did, too.

It was an elf! He was next door, pulling the string of lights from a tree!

"It's one of those . . . um . . . *kids!*" I explained.

The old man looked puzzled. "I can't see real well without my glasses . . . but he looks awful small to be a youngster."

"That's because—" John started, not sure of what he was going to say. He quickly continued. "—because he's . . . he's . . . standing in a snow bank! Come on Matt, let's get him!"

With that, we turned and ran across the yard, leaving old man Wentworth standing next to his house.

That had been a close one!

The elf scurried away from us and ran over top a parked car. He left tiny footprints in the snow that would be discovered soon enough by the car's owner. I wished I could be there when he sees those tiny footprints on the car!

John ran around one side of the car and I ran around the other. The elf bounded off the hood and took off across the lawn, but he wasn't fast enough. John is a good runner, and he easily overtook the small elf.

He leapt into the air and landed right on the tiny creature. The elf tried to get away but John grabbed him by the coat tail.

I pulled out my wand and touched the elf. Poof!

Whew. Only one more elf to go.

One more elf and one snow monster, that is.

"Come on!" I said to John. "I think I saw his tracks out there by the road!"

We walked back out into the street. It was getting kind of late, and I knew that soon I would have to go home. John too.

"We've got to find him," I said. We have to find the monster and that elf before tonight is over."

We were walking, looking around trees and houses, hoping to catch a glimpse of something.

Suddenly John stopped, pointing at the ground. He said nothing.

He didn't need to.

I saw what he was looking at, and it scared the daylights out of me.

A big red splotch stained the snow. There was a line of red splotches that trailed down the street.

Blood.

Had it happened? Had someone fallen prey to the snow monster?

I was horrified. And I felt terrible. I was responsible for bringing the snow monster to life. It was all my fault.

We had to know.

"Come on," I said to John.

"What?!?!?" he exclaimed.

"We have to follow the trail of blood," I told him. "It might lead us right to the snow monster."

"I'm not following any blood trail," John said defiantly, shaking his head. "If that thing has already eaten someone, who's to say that we won't be next?"

"Remember when we went camping in Cub Scouts?" I reminded him, "and you lost your flashlight in the woods? At night? Who helped you look for it?"

John had to think about that. Because I was the one who went out with him in the night, without a light, to help him find his flashlight. He hadn't wanted to go alone, so I agreed to go with him.

"Okay," he said, finally giving in. "But if we come across that . . . that . . . *thing* . . . I'm running like mad."

"Deal," I said.

Slowly, we began to follow the dark red stain through the snow.

In the glow of the streetlights, we continued following the dark red trail. There were broken Christmas decorations and lights everywhere. On the street, in yards . . . everywhere. I felt really bad for people who worked so hard to put them all up, only to have them torn down.

And it was all my fault! If I hadn't been playing around with that magic set, none of this would have happened.

But there was something else that worried me even more.

The trail of blood that we were following through the snow. Someone was bleeding. Bad.

"You know," John said, as we walked farther and farther. "Maybe we should call the police and let them handle this."

"Do you really think they'll believe us when we tell them that there's a snow monster on the loose?" I asked. "I mean . . . think about how you acted when I told *you* that the drawings on my poster had come to life. You didn't believe me. Do you think the police will?"

"No, probably not," John responded. "Probably not."

We pressed on. The snow continued to fall, and the wind began to blow harder. And it became *colder*. A storm was moving in.

Our boots squawked as we followed the dark red stain in the snow for what seemed like miles. Finally, the trail turned, went up a driveway, and up to a house.

The house was dark. There were no lights on inside.

John and I stopped, our eyes searching the

shadows for any signs of movement. We found none.

The trail of blood ran up the driveway and to the front door.

"Come on," I said quietly to John. He just shook his head from side to side.

"What's the matter?" I asked.

"I'm not going up there, huh-uh, no way, no sir," he said, all the while continuing to shake his head. What a chicken!

So I headed up the driveway.

Alone.

In the snow, I could see the dark red stain trail up the stone steps, across the porch —

— *to the door.*

What was worse, there was a dark red hand print on the wall just above the doorbell.

Oh no! This was not looking good.

A chill ran down my spine all the way to my toes. I have never been so frightened in all my life. Had it happened? Had it *really* happened? Had someone fallen victim to the snow monster? The snow monster that I created?

It was not a pleasant thought.

I turned to look at John. I wanted to call out to him, to tell him to come up to the porch, but even I was too afraid. I just stood there, looking at the bloody hand print, looking at the red stains on the porch and in the snow. I stood there for the longest time.

Until the door suddenly creaked open!

"Aaaaaauuuggggghhh!!" I screamed.

"Aaaaauuuuuuggggghhhh!!" a woman shrieked back. I don't know who was scared worse . . . me or her.

"What on earth are you doing here?" she demanded. She got over her fright quickly, and she sounded mad.

"I . . . I'm sorry, ma'am," I stammered.

"What on earth are you doing here?" she repeated.

"We . . . uh . . . we saw the blood in the

snow." I pointed to the ground. "We thought that someone might be hurt. We followed the trail of blood all the way from Willow Street."

The woman clicked on a porch light and looked at the snow by my feet. "Blood?" she asked. "Where?"

All at once she burst out laughing! She was laughing so hard that even I started giggling.

But I didn't know what was so funny.

"That's not blood!" she said. "It's only *ketchup!*" Again she laughed so hard she couldn't even talk. Finally, she spoke again.

"I was walking back from the market with my groceries. The plastic lid on a ketchup bottle broke, and the stuff leaked out of the plastic grocery bag. And you thought that it was blood?!?!"

Boy—was I embarrassed!! I'll bet my face was as red as the ketchup on the snow!

"I didn't notice it until I got half way up the driveway," she explained. "By then it was too late, and I wound up getting it all over my hands. I was just leaving again to go back to the store to get another bottle."

Ketchup! That's all that trail was. What relief! But then — something else bothered me.

"You're not walking to the store again, are you?" I asked. I was worried that she'd be out there all alone with that . . . that monster hanging around.

"Oh, heaven's no," she answered. "It's a little late for that now. I'm going to drive. But tell me . . . what are *you* doing out so late?"

"Oh, we're just . . . you know . . . playing, I guess."

"You're not responsible for tearing down everyone's Christmas ornaments and lights, are you?" she asked, cocking her head to the side and glaring at me.

"No, ma'am," I said. "But we're looking for them."

"You keep saying *'we'*," she said. "Who's *'we'*?"

"Me and —" I turned as I spoke, pointing to John.

Or I thought I was pointing to John. Because when I turned and looked to where

John had been standing just a few moments ago, he was gone!

Boy did I feel foolish. Foolish . . . and worried.

"Uh . . . um . . . well . . . ." I stammered. I didn't know what to say.

"Well, you'd better run along home," the woman ordered. "It's getting late. I'm sure your parents will be looking for you."

"Uh, sorry about . . . about thinking that the ketchup was blood," I said. "Sorry I scared you like that."

"Oh, thank you for being so concerned to check. That was very sweet."

She came outside and closed the door of her house behind her. I walked up the driveway as she got in her car and drove off.

When she was a ways up the road, I stopped walking.

"John?" I said loudly. "John? Where are you?"

My mind started racing. What if the snow monster had taken him? It was a horrible, horrible thought. I looked around.

No John.

I started to look for the huge tracks from the monster. I walked around houses and cars and garages. No monster tracks, and no sign of John, either.

"John?" I called out every so often. "Where did you go? John?"

I stopped under a streetlight. Now I wasn't really sure where I was. I had walked so long and so far that I was afraid that I had gotten lost. Traverse City isn't a huge city, but you can get lost just the same.

It was then that I looked down and saw the fresh tracks in the snow.

Monster tracks.

Now I was *really* afraid. I began to think that maybe the snow monster had eaten John, after all.

As I thought more and more about it, the less afraid I was . . . and the angrier I became.

What right did this snow monster have to be here, spoiling our Christmas? The elves and the reindeer and the snowman were bad enough. And they were only nuisances, anyway. The snow monster was big. He was ugly, because I drew him that way.

And something told me that he was dangerous. Very dangerous.

Still, the more I thought about it, the madder I became. I reached into my back pocket and pulled out my black magic wand, ready for battle.

"All right you super-sized overgrown long-haired white gopher," I whispered. *"Come on out. I'm ready for you."*

I followed the tracks the best I could. They wound around yards and houses, even around cars. I was sure that it would only be a matter of time before someone else spotted him.

Then what? They'd probably call out the army. They'd call out the Army and the Navy and the Air Force and the Marines and the National Guard. They'd probably call the Coast Guard, too.

And it would all be my fault.

I was getting tired, so I stopped near a parked car in a driveway.

Something moved over by the house. I could hear it shuffling around in the snow. And judging by the number of monster tracks around the yard, I figured it was him.

I *knew* it was him.

I held my wand out before me, inching closer toward the shadows.

Just one touch, I thought. *Just one touch and poof! He'd be gone. Then I could go home.*

I was sure that's where John was, too. I was certain that when the lady had come to the door he had ran. He had probably ran all the way home. He took off and ran when I needed him most!

Some help *he* turned out to be.

I walked slowly and carefully, arm outstretched, ready to send the snow monster back to my poster. My boots scrunched in the snow as I walked, and I tried to walk lighter. If I could surprise the snow monster, then it might make this thing a whole lot easier. If I could catch him off guard without him seeing me, then maybe — *maybe* — I had a chance.

I could hear him. The closer I got, I could actually hear the monster breathing. He was taking long, deep breaths . . . the kind of breaths you'd expect a snow monster to take.

Huuuuuuu . . . Hooooooooo . . . .

I slowly closed the gap between the shadows and me.

Huuuuuuu . . . Hooooooooo . . . .

My heart banged wildly in my chest, and I swallowed a big lump that had formed in my throat.

Closer . . . .

Huuuuuuu . . . Hooooooooo . . . .

I could hear the monster breathing louder. He was waiting for me, just around the corner of the house, waiting in the darkness.

Closer . . . .
Suddenly a dark form leapt out at me!

"*AAAAAUUUUUUUGGGGHHH!!!*" I screamed, waving the wand at the assailing snow monster.

"*AAAAAUUUUUUUGGGGHHH!!*" the snow monster screamed back.

Huh?

I was struck down, rolling on the ground in the darkness, fighting with—

The snow monster?

Hardly!

It was John!

"Ouch! Hey!" I yelled. "Get off me!"

"Matt?!?!? It's *you?!?!?*"

"Of course it's me!" I answered angrily.

"I thought you were the monster!" he said.

"I thought *you* were the monster," I responded, standing up and brushing the snow off my snow suit. I sure was glad that it was John. But he really had scared me. I think he scared *me* as much as I scared *him*.

"He's got to be around here somewhere," John said. "His tracks are everywhere."

We both stood in the shadows, looking out into the street. The snow continued to fall, and it glistened in the shining street lights. That's one thing that I really like about Traverse City . . . the winters are beautiful. That is, of course, if you like snow. Which I *do*.

Suddenly we saw him.

He was standing next to a tree on the other side of the street. He appeared to be looking the other way. I don't think he knew we were there.

Even facing the other way, he looked mean.

He looked *ugly*.

He looked like a snow monster.

"That's him!" I whispered. "That's my drawing! I mean . . . not my drawing . . . but — you know what I mean!"

"Holy cow," John said quietly. "Why did you have to make him so big?"

"I didn't! He just came that way."

The snow monster just stood there, standing next to the tree. Now I know what Yukon Cornelius went through in the *Rudolph* movie.

"Let's sneak up on him," I said. "If he's just standing there, looking the other way, maybe we can creep up on him without him knowing."

"I've got a better idea," John said. "Why don't you sneak up on him and I'll wait here. After all . . . he's your monster."

I didn't like that idea one bit.

"We'll both go," I said. "There's a better chance of touching him with the wand if we both go."

I didn't know if that was true or not, but I really wanted John to go with me.

"Okay," he whispered. "Let's go."

As we walked across the dimly lit street, it suddenly occurred to me how bizarre this whole situation was. Here I was, carrying a magic wand, crossing a street in Traverse City on a snowy December night, hoping to make a snow monster of my own creation disappear. Or at least go back to the poster where he belonged.

Some things are just too weird to try and understand.

We walked slowly across the street, our boots scrunching in the cold, new-fallen snow.

Scrunch. Scrunch-scrunch.

My eyes never left the hairy white form standing in the yard. He still had his back turned to us.

Scrunch.

I tried to walk quieter, but it was difficult in the snow.

Scrunch.

Scrunch-Scrunch.

It seemed to take us forever to reach the other side of the street. Finally, we stepped up over the snowy curb and trudged as quietly as we could to the sidewalk.

Now we were only a car length away from the snow monster.

He was huge! I have never seen any creature so big in my life. His hair was long and thick and white. It was so thick that I almost couldn't tell where his shoulders ended and his head began.

Scrunch.

We took another step closer.

Scrunch-scrunch. Two more steps.

I could feel my heart thumping in my

chest. It was so loud I thought for sure that the snow monster himself would be able to hear it.

John leaned close.

"You mean you actually have to touch that thing with your magic wand?" he asked.

I nodded.

"Can't you just wave it or something?"

I shook my head. *"The manual says that you have to actually touch the creation. When I tried just waving the wand at one of the elves, it created another one."*

John shuddered at the thought. The idea of not one, but *two* snow monsters running loose in Traverse City gave him the shivers.

I don't know how long we stood there, just staring at the hairy beast. I guess maybe I was hoping that he would just go away and maybe disappear on his own.

No such luck.

"Hurry up and get your wand and let's get this over with," John whispered nervously.

Actually, he was more than just *nervous*. He was terrified, just like I was.

I reached into the back pocket of my

snowsuit to grab the —

Oh no!

The magic wand! It was gone!

"What's wrong?" John asked, after a moment of fruitless searching in other pockets.

"My magic wand," I whispered. *"It's not there!"*

"What?!?!?" he exclaimed hoarsely. *"Check your other pockets!"*

"I did! It's not there! It must have fallen out when you tackled me!"

We both turned to look back at the shadowy area on the other side of the street.

"It must still be over there in the snow," I said.

We had no choice. We had to go back and get the wand.

Oh, how I wish I would have read that instruction manual before I started messing around with that magic kit!

I turned back around to make sure that the snow monster was still looking the other way.

He wasn't. He must have heard us

talking, because now he was facing us, his glaring red eyes glowing in the darkness.

We were face to face with the meanest, ugliest, nastiest, most gruesome creature that ever walked the face of the earth.

16

The snow monster was hideous. He was a hundred times worse than my drawing! I mean—I'm not really a good artist or anything. I just doodled the creatures on a piece of paper after school one day. I couldn't believe that in just a few minutes I had created the terrible beast in front of us!

He had two rows of sharp teeth, and two fangs hung down from either side of his mouth. Thick white hair covered his face, his chest, his whole body.

"Whh . . . wh . . . what . . . do . . . do . . . we . . . d-d-do . . . n-n . . . n-n-n . . . *now?*" John stammered. His whole body was shaking. Mine probably was, too . . . but I think I was too afraid to notice.

I didn't need to answer. The hulking snow monster took one step toward us and John and I both spun in our boots and began to run! We weren't hanging out around there any longer!

"Where are we going to go?!?!?" John screamed.

"I don't know!!!" I shouted back.

"How fast can he run?!?!?" John panted.

"I don't know that either!" I yelled back.

And I didn't. I didn't know anything about the snow monster except that he was big, mean, and ugly.

And he was after us.

I needed to get that magic wand back, and quick. John and I sprinted across the road and made a direct bee-line toward the corner of the house. We could hear the snow monster thundering behind us, but I dared not turn around.

"Oh no!" John shrieked, pointing ahead as he ran. "Look!"

In the snow near the corner of the house, the last elf that we had been trying to catch earlier had picked up the magic wand! He was holding it up in the air like it was some kind of great prize or something.

Have you ever had one of those days where just *nothing* seemed to go right?

"Hey!" I shouted. The elf suddenly looked up. "Give me that!"

The elf looked at me, looked at the wand—and ran!

He took off like a bolt of lightning!

Mischievous little bugger.

The tiny creature disappeared into the shadows, around the corner of the house.

"We're never going to catch him now!" John shouted. We were both running frantically, trying to out-distance the horrible creature behind us.

Now we were more worried about getting away from the snow monster than anything else.

Wand or no wand, we were in real danger.

Behind us, the monster let out a scream! It was a growling, unearthly shriek that echoed through the neighborhood. Maybe someone else would hear it and help us.

But then I would REALLY be in trouble!

We ran into someone's back yard. It was dark and hard to see. My boots sank deep into the snow, and running was almost impossible.

"Over there!" John shouted as we trudged through the snow. "Ally and Chris have been building a snow fort! We might be able to hide inside!"

Suddenly, I saw what he was talking about. A dark, dome-shaped shadow loomed before us. It looked like an igloo of some sort. It was hard to see in the dark.

"Other side!" John shouted. "Get on your hands and knees!"

John was the first to do so, and he found the small entrance to the fort. Soon his dark shape had disappeared. He was inside the igloo.

Suddenly the snow monster bounded around the side of the house! I didn't wait a moment longer, and fell instantly to my knees.

The opening was small and narrow but I was just able to squeak through. My snowsuit scraped the sides as I pulled myself forward on my elbows.

The inside of the igloo was dark, but John's form was even darker. I could see him on the other side of the igloo.

"Shhh," he whispered, and I froze. My breathing was heavy and I tried hard to calm down.

Had the snow monster seen us? Did he know where we were hiding?

We waited.

We waited some more.

Two minutes went by. Then three.

Suddenly we heard the crunching of heavy footsteps in the snow. They came closer.

Closer. . . .

Closer still—

They stopped.

He was right by the entrance of the igloo!

Could he smell us? Did he know we were there?

My worst fears were confirmed when a
dark shadow suddenly came over the entrance
of the igloo!

He was coming for us!

17

"AAAAUUUUGGGGHHH!!!" John and I both screamed. I crawled to the other side of the igloo. John and I screamed at the top of our lungs.

"HELP US!! SOMEBODY!! PLEASE HELP US!! HELP US!!"

"For crying out loud," an annoyed voice said. "Is that you, John? And Matt?"

Huh?

"Who's . . . who's there?" I asked.

"It's me. Chris. What are you guys doing

in my fort at night?"

Both John and I let out a sigh of relief. Chris was one year older than John and myself. I didn't know him real well, but he was pretty good friends with John.

"Chris!" John said. "Get in here! Quick! There's a monster after us!"

There was a long pause.

"Are you like . . . out of your minds or something?" Chris said. He wasn't all the way in the fort, and all we could see was the dark form of his shoulders and head.

"No, really!" I said. "He was chasing us just a few minutes ago! We had to come in here to get away!"

"I think you guys need a good shrink," Chris said. He clearly didn't believe us!

But could you blame him? I mean, if your friends told you that they had just been chased by an honest-to-goodness snow monster, would you believe *them?*

I didn't think so.

"I came out here because I thought I saw someone running in the yard," Chris said. "A couple of bigger kids from the other neighborhood tried to wreck our fort last week, and I just wanted to make sure it wasn't them. But you guys can hang out in here all you want—if you think it'll keep the monsters away." He laughed.

Ugh. I knew he wouldn't believe us.

"Chris," I began. "I'm serious. There's a snow monster that's running around Traverse City. You've got to get in here. Or get back in the house. It's too dangerous to be outside."

"Man, I thought I'd heard it all," he said, snickering. "A snow monster, eh? Yeah, I hate those things. All they do is cause problems."

He was making fun of me! Not only didn't he believe, me, but he thought this whole thing was one big joke!

"Chris, you gotta believe me," I said.

"Matt's right," said John. "There's a real snow monster out here. Matt brought it to life by accident. He's real and he's out here!"

"Well," Chris said. "I haven't seen any 'snow monsters' anywhere . . . but I do know that there's a couple of 'snow goofs' in my snow fort. I think that—"

Suddenly, Chris stopped talking . . . and started *screaming!!*

"Aagghhh!! It's got me!! Something's got me! Something's got me by the leg! *Agghhh!!!*"

Chris was being pulled out of the entrance!

"It's got my legs!! Help me! He's got me!! HE'S GOT *MEEEEE!!!!*" In the darkness, we could make out his helpless shape being pulled away! His arms were flailing about wildly as he screamed.

In the next instant, Chris was gone! He stopped screaming and we heard footsteps in the snow as the terrible creature took flight.

I had to stop him.

This was all my fault in the first place.

Now I knew for sure that the snow monster was not going to stop. He wouldn't stop, simply because there was probably no one who knew how to stop him.

Except me.

But to do it, I would have to get close enough to the snow monster to touch him with the wand. It seemed impossible.

I had to try. I couldn't bear the thought of the creature taking Chris like that. If I didn't stop him now, how many other kids would he get?

True, I didn't have the magic wand, but the thought of just doing *nothing* was unbearable.

"Come on!" I shouted to John. "We've got to stop him! We have to save Chris from the snow monster!"

"Where are you going?!?!?" he demanded. "You can't go after that . . . that *thing!!!*"

"We have to, John. At least . . . *I* have to. I brought him to life. I created him. I've got to stop him. *Somehow.*"

Somehow.

Reluctantly, John agreed.

"All right. I'll go."

We scrambled out of the igloo and took off across the yard, and it was too dark in the back yard to see any tracks. I wasn't sure which way the monster had traveled, but it sounded like he had headed toward the other side of the house. If that were the case, we would probably be able to see him in the glow of the streetlights.

"ROOOOAAAARRR!!!"

The loud growl came from right in front of me! I was so shocked I fell backwards, stumbled, and landed in the snow. John had been right behind me, and he tripped over and fell. He fell forward and landed on top of me!

Laughter.

Lots of laughter.

Chris.

"Hahahahahahah!!" he laughed, doubling over in delight. "Wow! Did I get you guys good! I really got you good!"

"Thanks," I sneered, getting to my feet. "Thanks a *lot.*"

I brushed the snow off, and John did the

same as he stood up.

"There really is a snow monster loose," John said with annoyance in his voice.

"Yeah, sure," Chris replied. "He's probably big and hairy and has fangs or something, huh? I think you guys have watched too many Christmas specials on TV."

"Come on," I said to John, ignoring Chris's rude comments. "We have to find him."

"Hey," Chris said as we walked away. "You can use my fort to get away from the monster anytime you want." More laughter.

The jerk.

"And you're a *'friend'* of his?" I asked John.

"Awww, Chris really isn't so bad," John replied. "But you have to admit . . . being chased by a snow monster isn't something many people are going to believe."

"They'll believe it when all of a sudden people come up missing. There's no telling *what* that monster is capable of."

We continued walking through the snow, through backyards and driveways. The snow monster's tracks were everywhere! He was really covering a lot of ground.

Suddenly, a small dark form darted across the street in front of us. At first I thought it was a dog, but it wasn't.

It was the elf!

I could see him still carrying the magic wand!

"Get him!" I shouted, and John and I took flight.

We were off!

The elf saw us and tried to run to the other side of the street, but we were gaining on him. He was fast, but not as fast as us.

"There he goes!" I cried. "Around the car!"

There was a parked car in a driveway and the little creature ran around to the other side. John went one way and I went the other.

Not fast enough! We almost had him, but he sped up the driveway and we chased him along side the house.

"He's headed for the backyard!" John shouted.

We were in hot pursuit. The little elf bounded over a snowbank and raced through the snow. He could really move fast when he wanted to, that was for sure.

Here in the yard it was easier for the elf to run than it was for us. The snow came up to our knees and we sank quickly. The elf was nimble and light and could run on top of the snow without a problem. We could see his shadowy form as he raced on, heading for the next yard.

Suddenly he stopped!

What was he doing?

He was stopped in the middle of the yard. It was easy to see his dark shape against the white canvas of snow.

What was he doing?

We kept up our pace until we were only a few feet away.

"What's he doing?" John whispered. *"How come he's not running?"*

The elf looked confused. He turned and looked at us, then he turned and looked away.

That's when we saw it. Both John and I let out a gasp.

The elf wasn't confused — it was scared!

When I took another look, I could see why.

It was the snow monster. He was on the other side of the elf, about twenty feet away. I could see his hulking dark shape in the darkness.

It was a stand off.

What would happen?

What could we do?

We desperately needed to get the wand from the elf. If I lunged forward, I might be able to wrestle the magic wand from the elf. But if I missed, the snow monster would surely tear me limb from limb.

What a horrible thought.

Now what, Mr. Magician? I thought, mentally scolding myself.

Some magician I turned out to be.

I suddenly decided that I would have to take my chances.

I *had* to have that magic wand back. There was just no other way.

The elf turned to look at the snow

monster.

Now was my chance.

I sprang.

The movement caught the little elf totally by surprise. He turned and saw my shape lunging toward him, but it was too late for him to do anything. I fell on top of him, and we both fell into the deep snow. My hands instantly began searching for the magic wand.

The elf squirmed and wiggled and tried to get away, but I held him in the snow. I searched frantically for the—

Ah ha!

I found it! It was —

Broken! Oh no! The magic wand had snapped in half! It must've broken when I landed on the elf! Sure enough, the elf must have touched the tip, because in the next instant, he vanished. But he must have landed on top of the wand! It had snapped in half! Now what would we do?!?!?

Meanwhile, John was scared stiff. He just stood there, watching the huge snow monster. Only a split second had passed since I tackled the elf, and now John looked at me holding the broken wand.

"You broke the wand?!?!?" John cried. "Will it still work?"

I wasn't sure. Maybe it would, maybe it wouldn't.

There was only one way to find out.

I turned and faced the enormous white beast looming only a few yards away.

Now or never.

In a sudden rush, I charged toward the snow monster, holding out the broken wand before me.

I was either very, very brave . . . or totally crazy. Now I know how David felt when he went up against Goliath. As I got closer to the snow monster, his huge shape loomed over me. He was even bigger than I'd imagined!

But the creature turned and ran! I mean — I think I actually saw fear in his red eyes! It was as if he knew that the wand would destroy him.

But he didn't go far. He stopped in the next yard and turned back, watching us. He just stood there, his red eyes glowing in the darkness.

In the next instant he turned and ran again. I could see his huge, dark shape leaping over fences and bounding through yards. Soon he was out of sight, lost somewhere in the dozens of homes that dotted the neighborhood.

"Why did he do that?" John asked.

All I could do was shake my head. "I don't know," I answered. "Maybe he was afraid of the wand. Maybe he knows that it will send him back to my poster."

We both just stood there for a moment, the cold snow blowing against our faces. Finally, John spoke.

"Now what?" he asked quietly.

"We go get him," I said bravely. Or, I tried to sound brave. Now that I knew the monster was afraid of the magic wand, I wasn't as scared as I was before. I had a trump card. An ace in the hole.

"You're crazy," John said.

"You're probably right," I agreed. "But if you tell anyone that you saw a snow monster in Traverse City, they'll say you're crazy, too. So what do you want to be . . . crazy with me or crazy all by yourself?"

John had to think about that for a moment.

"Well," he finally said. "I guess I'm with you. I can't let you go up against that thing all by yourself."

"Fine," I said. "What time is it?"

John has one of those watches that glow in the dark. He took off his glove and rolled up his jacket sleeve. I could see the blue glow from where I stood.

"Seven o'clock," he said.

"I have until nine. If I'm not home by then I'm gonna be in a lot of trouble."

"Same here," John said.

We both looked across the darkened yards, the streets lit by yellow lights. Snow was beginning to fall harder. It does that a lot during a Traverse City winter. Being right on Lake Michigan causes what is called 'lake effect' snow, which can dump a few inches on the ground in just a few hours.

"We'll need a flashlight," I said. "There's no telling where the monster went. We'll have to follow his tracks."

"My dad has a flashlight in the garage," John offered. "I can go get it."

We were only a block away from John's house, so we trudged back there and he retrieved the light from the garage. It was one of those big lantern flashlights . . . the real powerful ones. I shined it up into the sky, into the falling snow. The white beam pierced the night like a laser.

"Come on," I said. "It's snowing harder. If we don't get going now, his tracks will be covered with snow."

Armed with only a broken wand and a flashlight, we set off into the night to hunt for the snow monster.

The tracks wound through yards and out of the neighborhood. At one point, the beast crossed the highway. We picked up his tracks on the other side.

We followed the snow monster's footprints through the Open Space, which is kind of a big park area by the bay. In the summer we swim and play volleyball there.

But besides the tracks, we didn't see any sign of the monster. We walked and walked, following the huge footprints through the snow.

"This is crazy," John said as we followed the tracks through an empty, darkened parking lot. "Isn't he ever going to stop?"

"He's a snow monster," I said, watching the footprints in the flashlight beam. "He can probably walk for days and days."

It was really snowing hard now, and the monster's footprints were becoming more and more clouded with puffy white powder. We would have to find the snow monster fast or risk never finding him at all.

We stopped walking, and John swept the flashlight beam across the parking lot. The beam was cut short by dark buildings and large tree trunks. Empty shadows, obscured by the falling snow, glared back at us.

But still no snow monster.

By now, we were dangerously close to downtown. I say 'dangerously' because that's what it was. I couldn't bear the thought of the monster running wild and loose down Front Street. What would happen to the innocent people out shopping for Christmas gifts? The thought of the hideous white creature bounding through downtown Traverse City gave me the chills.

We started off again. The heavy snow pounded at our face and the wind whipped against us. It was blowing so hard now that even the sounds of the city — cars, trucks, a few horns now and then — were completely drowned out. All we could hear was the wind.

The trail became harder and harder to see. The newly fallen snow, blown and cast about by the wind, had covered up the last of the tracks. Finally, it became impossible to see any sign of the monster's footprints.

We stopped. Neither John nor I spoke. The lake effect snowfall was rapidly becoming an all-out winter storm, and we didn't know where to go from here.

We were in a large field at the edge of Lake Michigan. The water wasn't frozen yet; that would come in January. I could hear the crashing waves hitting the snowy, icy shoreline.

I swept the flashlight in front of us. Small whitecaps in the bay licked upward and disappeared. To the left of us, further down the shore . . . nothing.

To the right of us, twenty feet away . . . .

The snow monster.

21

We didn't see him at first. It was snowing and blowing too hard, and the flashlight beam could hardly penetrate the curtain of snow whipping in from the tossing lake.

John and I both spotted him at the same time. He was standing still, like he was waiting for us.

A lump formed in my throat and I could feel my heart begin to pound harder in my chest.

The monster's red eyes began to glow brighter and brighter. It was creepy. The wind blew his white hair all around. His mouth was open and I could again see his enormous, razor-sharp teeth.

My hand reached for the broken wand in the back pocket of my snowsuit. I pulled it out and held it before me.

The creature suddenly let out a chilling howl! It scared both John and I, and I felt like running. I wanted to run. To turn and run as fast as my legs could carry me, over the new fallen snow, across Front Street, back to my neighborhood. Back to my home. Climb in bed, wake up tomorrow. In the morning it would all be a bad dream. In the morning, I would wake up and remember the dream, and I would laugh and forget about it. Yep . . . tomorrow morning, all of this would just be a dream.

But right now it was a nightmare.

I decided not to wait a moment longer. If I did, I might not get another chance.

I handed John the flashlight.

"Okay," I said. "One . . . ."

I counted slowly out loud.

"Two . . . ."

I took a deep breath.

"Three!"

I attacked.

Waving the wand furiously in front of me I charged, trudging through the snow.

The snow monster didn't run this time. As I drew close he howled a sickening, gruesome screech. It was the sound of metal on metal, the squealing of tires locked up on pavement. It was horrible.

Suddenly I was upon him . . . or about 'upon' him as much as I could . . . especially when he was twelve feet tall!

The next thing I knew I was sent flying, tumbling through the snow. I was disoriented and confused.

What had happened? Obviously the creature had struck me . . . but had I been able to touch him with the wand? Had he disappeared?

"Matt?!?!?" I heard John yell.

"I'm okay!" I shouted, getting back to my feet. When I looked back I realized that my efforts to use the wand had been in vain.

I could see the monster in the flashlight

beam. He was thundering toward me. In the next second he would be—

I dove sideways, but the monster struck me with a powerful blow from his arm. I heard an awful tearing and realized that my snowsuit had been ripped open.

Better my suit than me!

I stood up once again, prepared for the fight of my life. This monster was not going to win. I wouldn't let him.

And then—

An opportunity. The huge creature suddenly seemed confused. He was facing John, who was still frozen in his boots, aiming his light at the horrendous creature.

The light! It was blinding the snow monster!

It was the break I needed.

I charged after the creature with all my might, the magic wand leading the way.

But the creature had his own ideas. He didn't like the beam of light in his face, and it made him mad.

Suddenly the creature sprang forward,

arms outstretched.

He was going for the light! He was going to attack John!

22

I knew I had to reach the monster before he got to John.

I *had* to.

John screamed in terror as the creature shot toward him. He dropped the flashlight and it went out. Now it was *really* dark.

But I could see the snow monster. He was right in front of me, right there . . . .

Almost . . . .

Now!

The creature lunged at John as I swung

my arm forward.

Suddenly, John screamed! Oh no! Was I too late?

"No you don't!" I hollered at the top of my lungs. "No . . . you . . . *DON'T!*"

"Stop it! Hey! That hurts!"

It was *John*.

I was on top of him, my arms around him, grinding the wand into his rib cage.

"Man, that hurt," he said.

I drew back, confused.

Where was the snow monster? I knew he had been there. I had felt his wiry, furry coat against my face. I could feel his body heat. And he stunk, too. He smelled like our dog when he stays outside in the rain.

I looked all around in the darkness, listening for the monster. If he had gotten away, I'm sure we would have heard his heavy footsteps pounding through the snow.

But the snow monster was gone.

I leapt to my feet.

"It worked!" I shouted. "It really worked!"

But no sooner had I said those words than something very strange began to happen.

The sky began to lighten. Not like sunshine, but it began to whiten. It became brighter and brighter. The snow stopped.

Suddenly there was nothing around us but white. Bright, bright white.

What on earth is going on?

"Matt . . . what happened? Where are we?"

I couldn't answer him. I didn't know myself. All I could do was stare.

All around us was nothing but white. I couldn't see any ground, but obviously it had to be there. But there was no sky, no trees, no city, no buildings.

It was then that I knew. It was then that I realized what had happened.

The wand. It was broken, and somehow it wasn't working properly.

When I touched the snow monster, I succeeded in sending the creature back to the paper. Back to nothing but my imagination.

But I had also touched myself with the

white tip. And John as well.

Now we too had been sent to this strange world. A world that — until now — existed only in my mind, only on a single sheet of white paper.

Now John and I found ourselves in this bizarre realm, a universe of nothing but white.

A paper world.

But we were about to find out that we were not alone.

You may find it hard to imagine a world of nothing but white . . . and yet, that is what lay before us. As our eyes adjusted to the intense brilliance, we began to make out shapes and forms.

We were in a desert! I could make out rolling dunes and valleys, all perfectly white. But it didn't seem to be sand, or even snow for that matter. At our feet was a dusty powder that seemed more like fine pollen than anything else. There was a sky, but it was a soft, creamy white.

John and I both stared for the longest time. Neither one of us spoke a word.

"Where are we?" John finally asked.

"I think we're in my poster," I said, looking around.

"You mean . . . now we're a part of your drawing? With the elves and the reindeer and the snowman and—"

"—And the snow monster," I said, nodding.

"Where in the world did you get a magic kit that does this sort of stuff?" he asked. "I mean . . . it should be illegal!"

"It was a Christmas gift from my Grandma and Grandpa," I answered. We were both still gazing around in amazement, staring into a sea of white. For as far as we could see, there was nothing but white. Empty, blank white. No hills, no trees. No houses, no sky. Just . . . *white.*

"What now?" John asked.

I shook my head. "I don't—"

Suddenly I remembered! I had the manual in my pocket! The manual from the magic kit!

I unzipped the pocket and thrust my hand in it, expecting not to find it. I was afraid that maybe somehow, somewhere, during all of the excitement, I had lost it.

My hand found the thick paper book. It was there!

"What?" John asked. "What have you got?"

"The manual from my magic kit!" I answered excitedly. "Maybe it will tell us what to do!"

John leaned toward me, staring down at the book as I flipped it open to the beginning.

"*Professional Stage Magician Magic Kit,*" I read aloud. "*Table of contents.*"

"There!" John pointed. At the tip of his finger was this sentence:

IN CASE OF EMERGENCY - PAGE 72

I quickly thumbed through the book. The 'emergency' section was the very last part. In fact, page 72 was the very last page.

"If you are reading this page," I read aloud, *"it is most certainly because you did NOT read the manual before trying to perform any magic."*

How true.

"If this is the case," I continued to read aloud, *"repeat the following word FOUR times. NOTICE: THIS IS FOR EMERGENCIES ONLY!"*

"What's the word?" John asked. I pointed to it, but I didn't say it. It was typed in huge letters:

MAAZ-AK-EEL-A

"Huh?" John asked. "What is that supposed to mean?" I just shook my head. How should I know? I didn't read the manual. Maybe if I did, I'd know what the strange word meant.

But then again, if I'd have read the manual, we wouldn't be in the kind of trouble we were!

Suddenly John snapped his fingers. "Hey!" he said. "That's it! That word is

'Aleekazaam' . . . only it's backwards!"

I looked at the word on the paper.

John was right! That's exactly what it was!

"All we have to do is repeat it four times," I said.

"Just like the movie *Beetlejuice*," John said.

I looked around. There was still nothing but a thick white sheet. Everywhere I looked — nothing but white.

"Ready?" I asked.

John nodded. "Give it a try."

I took a deep breath.

"Maaz-ak-eel-a" I said once. "Maaz-ak-eel-a."

Twice.

The ground beneath us started to shake.

"Maaz-ak-eel-a," I said again.

Three times. The trembling grew stronger. I took another deep breath, paused, looked at John, and then looked back at the manual.

"Maaz-ak-eel-a," I finished.

The ground beneath us fell away! The

bright white seemed to tear open, and the air was filled with a tremendous thundering sound.

We were falling!

24

Both John and I screamed and kicked wildy in the air. We were falling, tumbling head over heels, through a pure white blanket.

"What's happening?!?!?!" John screamed.

"I don't know!" I shouted back.

"Oh come now, come now, don't be silly," a voice said. It wasn't John's voice . . . and it most certainly wasn't *my* voice!

Then I realized that we didn't seem to be falling after all . . . it was more like we were floating. Almost like we were flying.

"Who . . . who's there?" John stammered.

Before us, a gray image was materializing! It was coming toward us! It was a large shape, the size of a grown man, and as it drew closer, it became darker.

Then I knew! We were in some sort of mist, some kind of fog. The form coming toward us was indeed a man, and now I could make out his legs and arms. He walked right out of the white mist like he was emerging from a cloud.

"Tell me something," John whispered. *"Is he one of your drawings?"*

"No," I whispered back. *"I didn't draw him."*

Now the man was right in front of us, only a few feet away. He was dressed all in black, and it was very obvious that this man was, I was sure, a magician. He had a magician's hat and a cape. He had a thick, dark mustache and a beard, and he leaned on a cane as he stared at us.

"Yes, yes, what is it?" he asked.

"Uh . . . ." It was all I could say.

"Please," he said sternly. "I haven't got all day. What seems to be the problem?"

"Who are you?" I managed to ask.

"I am the Great Garbonzo," he said proudly, tipping his hat and bowing forward a little bit. "At your service. And of what service to you may I be?"

"Well, we're kind of in a lot of trouble," I said. He listened intently as I told him how I had accidentally brought the elves and the reindeer and the snowman to life. When I told him about the snow monster, he shuddered.

"You mean," he said after I finished, "that this creature is running loose? It's *still* running loose?"

"Yeah, I think so," I said, nodding my head. John nodded his head too.

"My, my, my, that *is* a problem," he said softly, stroking his beard. "A big problem indeed."

"Where are we?" I asked, looking around again. I still could see nothing but the white clouds that swirled all around us.

"You are in the Secret Mist," he replied.

133

"This is my home."

"What's the 'Secret Mist'?" John asked.

"The Secret Mist is a special realm between magic and reality. You see, magic and reality cannot mix. If something is real, then it cannot be magic. If something is magic, then it cannot be real. For magic to be allowed in the 'real' world, it must travel through the Secret Mist. Understand?"

"Well, I guess so," I answered. But there were a lot of things that had happened that I didn't understand!

"Well, what do we have to do to send the snow monster back to my poster?" I asked. "And fix everyone's Christmas trees and lights and ornaments?"

The magician nodded as he answered. "I'm afraid we'll have to go back to the real world and fix things one by one," he said. "Including your snow monster."

"Can't you just wave your wand or something and make everything right?" John asked.

The Great Garbonzo looked at him for a

moment, and then burst out laughing!

"Oh, I'm afraid it's not that simple," he said, still chuckling. "But I do hear that a lot. Everyone thinks that things can be fixed with a simple wave of a magic wand — but that's just not the way things work. You see, once you've brought creatures through the Secret Mist, they DO become real. I'm sure you read that in the manual that came with the magic kit."

"Umm," I stuttered. "I, uh, I kind of . . . well, I guess I really didn't read the manual."

"You didn't read the manual and you began performing magic?!?!" He looked angry.

Boy, was my face red!

"Yes, sir," I said, hanging my head. "I'm really sorry." And I meant it. I really *was* very sorry.

"Well, there's nothing so bad that can't be fixed with a little magic," he said. "A little magic . . . and a lot of hard work. I suppose we should get started."

And with that, he took off his hat and held it out before him.

"Jump in," he ordered.

Huh?

John and I just stared at him, every second or two glancing down at the top hat that he held in his hands.

"Well?" he asked.

"You want us to do *what*?" I replied.

"Jump in the hat. Go on. Just jump in."

"You mean like . . . just jump in?"

"Oh, I know it looks impossible, but remember, your are in the Secret Mist. Many things that may seem strange to you here are in fact, quite possible. Just dive into the hat like you would jump off of a diving board. I assure you, no harm will come."

John shook his head and looked at me. "You first, Matt," he said. John felt the same way that I did. Diving into a black hat is not something you do every day.

"Well, here goes nothing," I whispered, and I looked at John, then at the Great Garbonzo, then at the hat.

"Come on, come on," the magician said. "Time is wasting. You're not the only people I have to help, you know. I'm a very busy magician."

Here goes nothing, I said once again to myself.

I crouched down, sprang up, and dived into the hat.

In the next instant I was back in Traverse City! It was still snowing madly, and the wind was howling.

But I was alone!

I stood in the dark for a moment, waiting and watching. I had no idea where the snow monster might be, and right now I didn't *want* to know.

Suddenly John was standing next to me! He just kind of 'popped' up! It was strange. In the next instant, the Great Garbonzo was there, too.

"You're going to freeze," I told him. He didn't have a coat or a hat or gloves or anything.

"Oh, I don't think so," he said, and he made one swoop of his cane over his head. "Azzam!" he shouted.

Nothing happened. Or, at least, it *looked* like nothing happened.

"What did you do?" John asked.

"I've placed an invisible wall of warm air around me. No snow or wind can get through. It's quite toasty, actually."

Too cool! I wished I could do that!

"But let's get to the business at hand," he continued. "Where was the last place you saw this snow monster?"

I explained that I had charged the monster and he had disappeared.

"Ah yes, ah yes," he said. "Quite possible. He must be around here somewhere. We'll probably find him near the place where he came from. Tell me . . . where is your poster?"

"My poster?" I asked. It's in my—" But I couldn't finish the sentence.

The poster was in my bedroom!

"You mean that the snow monster will try to get back into my poster?!?!?!" I stammered.

"I'm afraid so," the magician answered. "Sooner or later, he'll become bored with all of his mischief. He'll want to return to where he came from."

Oh no!

What if he tried to return to my poster tonight? Would he break into the house? Would anyone get hurt?

This whole thing was way out of control!

"Come on," I said, starting to jog. "I'll take you there!"

We ran back through the Open Space and through downtown, then down a few more blocks to our street.

"There," I said, pointing. We slowed down. "That's my house, right over there."

The Great Garbonzo stopped and looked.

"My, just look at this neighborhood," he said, shaking his head. "It looks like a tornado went through here."

And it did, too. Christmas trees had been

141

knocked over, strings of lights lay in yards, broken bulbs were scattered in the street. Everyone's house had suffered some damage at the hands of the elves, reindeer, snowman, and the snow monster.

"Well, some of this won't be a problem at all," the magician said, and with a single wave of his cane a Christmas tree righted itself! The string of lights that had been torn off came alive, winding itself back around the tree like a snake. Broken Christmas tree bulbs suddenly snapped up from the ground and set themselves perfectly on the tree.

"Awesome!" John exclaimed. And it was! The Great Garbonzo waved his cane again and the repairs continued.

"Hey!" John said. "When you get done here, can you do my bedroom?"

Great idea, but something told me that the answer would be 'no'!

It only took a few minutes for the entire block to be repaired. All of the lights were strung along the rooftops, the trees had been set up straight, and even the broken ornaments were fixed.

It would've taken John and I *days* to do all that—but it only took the Great Garbonzo five minutes! He even fixed the tear in my snowsuit, which was a good thing. I didn't know how I would've explained that to Mom!

"There," the magician said finally, admiring his own handiwork. "Much better. Now . . . on to—"

"LOOK OUT!" John screamed at the top of his lungs. "IT'S HIM!! IT'S THE SNOW MONSTER!"

26

He was right.

We hadn't been watching, and the snow monster had crept up right behind us! He was charging!

I leapt and turned and he missed me by inches.

The Great Garbonzo wasn't so fortunate. The huge white beast knocked him to the ground and they both fell, tumbling into the snow.

What would we do?!?!? What *could* we

do?!?!?

Suddenly, the snow monster was on his feet again. The Great Garbonzo seized the opportunity and rolled sideways, away from the creature. The snow monster turned and looked at John and I, then burst off, disappearing behind a house. He was gone.

We ran to help the Great Garbonzo to his feet.

"Are you okay?" I asked. He looked a bit shaken.

"Yes, I think I'm fine," he replied, brushing the snow from his cape. "I think I'm—" He stopped, suddenly looking down in the snow.

"My cane! Where is my cane?!?!?!"

We looked and looked, but we couldn't find it.

"Without my cane, most of my magic is gone!" he exclaimed. And he was right. The invisible wall of warm air that had surrounded him was gone, and now snowflakes were falling on him. And he was shivering.

"You're going to freeze to death," John

said.

"Maybe so," the magician replied. "But right now, we have a bigger problem. I must get that cane back. Brrr . . . it's *cold!*"

"We can't go searching for your cane or the snow monster until you get something warm," I said.

Suddenly I had an idea!

"Hey! Wait here. I'll go inside my house and get my dad's snowmobile suit and his boots. They'll probably fit you."

I dashed off and returned a few minutes later. He slipped into the snowmobile suit, which was a little big for him, but the boots fit perfectly. I even borrowed Dad's warm hat and a pair of gloves.

"Thank you," the magician said. "Now—let's find that horrible creature."

"We'd better hurry," I said. "It's getting late. Let's follow the snow monster's footprints until we catch up with him."

We were off. The three of us traveled through back yards, across roads and into the next block. We had to be getting close.

The Great Garbonzo had been walking behind us, and now he stopped.

"What's that?" he said, pointing.   I followed his arm and looked in the direction that he was pointing. I could see flashing red and blue lights. Just then, I could hear the blare of a siren.

"Oh no!" John said. "We're too late! Something terrible has happened!"

"Come on!" I urged, and started running through the snow toward the commotion.

We stayed in the shadow of a large house and peered around the corner. There were three police cars, lights spinning, parked on the street. Another police car was in the driveway of a house. Uniformed policemen in heavy blue coats milled about.

"I'll go up and find out what's going on," I said. "You guys stay out of sight."

As I emerged from the shadows, one of the officers spotted me, and then another. Apparently, they weren't too concerned about me, because they went right back to their own business. I could hear a woman talking to one of the policemen.

"It was *horrible*," she was saying. "It was huge . . . the size of a bear. Bigger than a bear! And white! It had glowing red eyes, and—"

I didn't pay attention to anything else. I walked over to where one of the policemen was standing.

"Um, excuse me," I stammered. "What happened?"

The officer smiled and looked at me, glanced at the woman on the other side of the street, and then looked back at me.

"Snow monster," he said, rolling his eyes. "She says she saw a snow monster in her front yard. A snow monster with a cane." He chuckled a little. "You haven't seen anything like that running around, have you, young fella?" He smiled.

This was it. I couldn't lie to a policeman! Besides . . . this whole thing had gotten out of control. Maybe if I told him, we could catch the monster. Sure, I'd probably get in BIG trouble, but maybe they could help. Maybe we could stop the snow monster before he hurt anyone.

"Yes sir, I have seen him," I answered somberly. "I'm afraid I created him. I drew him on a poster and brought him to life with my magic kit." I hung my head, waiting for the worst.

"Well, isn't that nice," he said, smiling. "Do you always make up stories like that?"

He didn't believe me!

"Stories?!?!?" I exclaimed. "It's not a story! It's true!"

"Sure it is, sure it is," he said, walking away.

I followed him.

"Honest!" I said. "It's true! I made him come alive, along with a bunch of elves and reindeer! We got rid of them, but the snow monster is still out there!"

"Of course it is," the policeman said. "Along with flying saucers and bigfoot and a bunch of other monsters. Now you run along. We've all got things to do. *Better* things to do than chase some 'snow monster'." He walked away.

I ran back to find John and the Great Garbonzo on the other side of the house.

"Well?" asked the magician.

"A woman says she saw him! He has your cane!"

"Well, at least we know for sure that he has it," he said. "Come on. We've got to find him. We've got to find him before he figures out how to use the cane."

And so we were off again. We had lost the tracks of the snow monster, but we weren't willing to give up just yet. We searched through back yards and empty fields, behind garages and under trees. We looked high and low, but couldn't find the snow monster.

"Let's go back to your house, Matt," the Great Garbonzo said to me. "It's our best chance to find him. We'll never find him in this blizzard."

The Great Garbonzo was right. It was snowing much harder now, and the wind was howling like a banshee. I don't know what a banshee was, but that's what my dad always said when the wind was blowing hard. He said it was 'howling like a banshee'.

We took some shortcuts through some yards and returned home, but we didn't see any sign of the snow monster.

Until I looked up at my bedroom window.

He was there.

In the window.

In my bedroom.

How he got there, I could only guess. I was horrified.

"The cane," the magician said. He sounded worried. "He's learning to use the cane. We must stop him. At any cost, he must be stopped."

"How did he get in my bedroom?" I asked. "I mean . . . Mom and Dad would have seen him for sure. Or else—" I stopped talking, and a wave of horror rushed over me.

"No, look!" John said. He pointed to our living room window.

Mom was sitting in a chair, reading a magazine. Dad was poking at the fire in the fireplace. They were okay.

At least for the moment.

"He used the magic cane to get to your bedroom," the Great Garbonzo said. "He knows that that's where your poster is. He's trying to go back."

"Why can't we just let him?" I asked. "Isn't that where we want him to be, anyway?"

The magician looked at me. It was obvious that he was very worried.

"If he goes back to your poster by using the cane," he said, "then there is nothing stopping him from coming back. He will use the cane to go back and forth, through the Secret Mist, whenever he wants. Not only that, he can bring many other creatures with him. If he goes back to your poster using the cane, we will *never* be able to stop him."

I looked back up at the bedroom window. The snow monster was still there, but he was moving slowly, like he was looking for something.

There was still time. There was still time to stop him, to prevent him from going back into the poster.

"So, now what?" John asked.

"We go after him," the Great Garbonzo said. "It is the only way."

We walked to the front door of our house.

"How are we going to get upstairs without your Mom and Dad finding out?" John asked.

Good question. I had to think about that for a minute. Then I had an idea!

"All three of us will go into the house. John, you and mister—I mean, Great Garbonzo—you both hide in the foyer behind the door, just in case Mom or Dad comes. They probably won't, but just in case. I'll go into the living room and talk to them for a few minutes. That's when you guys will sneak upstairs."

"What about your little sister?" John

asked. "She's a pest!"

"Kimmy's asleep. She went to bed an hour ago, I'm sure. And Rusty sleeps in her bedroom, so we don't have to worry about the dog barking."

"All right," John agreed. "If you think it will work."

"It *has* to work," I said quietly. "It just has to."

"There is no more time to waste," the Great Garbonzo said. "We must hurry."

I stepped up onto the porch and opened the door.

29

The moment I walked in the house I called out to Mom and Dad.

"I'm home!" I shouted, quickly taking off my snowsuit and boots. John and the Great Garbonzo slid silently inside. Here in the light, I caught a better look at the magician. Boy, did he look funny! The snowsuit didn't quite fit him, and he looked more like a cartoon character than a man!

"Hide behind the door over there," I whispered. They both did as I said. I took out

the broken magic wand and the manual and stuffed them in my jeans pocket. I hung up my snowsuit and glanced at John and the magician behind the door.

"I'm going to go talk to Mom and Dad. When you hear me talking to them, sneak upstairs." They both nodded their heads in understanding.

The TV was on. Mom was still reading her magazine, and Dad was watching the news.

"Hey guys," I said.

Dad looked up from the TV and Mom lowered her magazine. We talked for a minute or two, Dad asked me if I'd finished my homework (which I had), and Mom said that there were fresh chocolate-chip cookies on the kitchen counter. Yum!

"I'm going to go upstairs and listen to my CD's," I announced. Mom glanced at the clock on the wall. It was eight-thirty.

"For fifteen minutes," she said. "Then it's shower time."

I shrugged. "Sure, Mom," I said, and walked back to the foyer. I peered behind the door.

No John, no Great Garbonzo.

They made it! I hadn't even heard them myself.

I walked quickly down the hall, turned, and went upstairs. Sure enough, John and the magician were waiting for me.

The three of us tiptoed to my bedroom door. I couldn't believe that the snow monster was actually in there! I figured that he would be making an incredible racket, and that Mom and Dad surely must have heard him. But behind the closed bedroom door, there wasn't much noise at all. Just a kind of scuffling sound.

"Oh, how I wish I had my cane right now," the Great Garbonzo said quietly.

"And I wish I hadn't broke my magic wand," I said in reply, pulling the two pieces from my pocket.

"A wand!?!?!?!" the magician exclaimed. "You have the wand?!?!?!"

"Well, yeah," I said. "But I broke it when I fell. I can't get it to work." I held it out, and the Great Garbonzo took the two pieces in his hand. He fitted the broken ends together.

Suddenly a golden glow formed around the wand! It was as if it was surrounded by fire.

"*Azzam,*" the Great Garbonzo whispered, closing his eyes as he spoke.

The two pieces of the wand stuck together! It worked! John and I looked at the wand in amazement. There was no crack, nothing that would indicate that the wand had even been broken.

The Great Garbonzo smiled.

"Now," he said triumphantly. "Let's go get my cane back . . . and send that snow monster back to your poster."

I took a step toward the door and placed my hand on the knob. When I hesitated, the Great Garbonzo nodded.

"*Go ahead,*" he whispered. "*We must hurry.*"

I held my breath, slowly turned the knob, and opened the door.

30

The door swung open, and the scuffling that we had heard moments before suddenly stopped.

It *knew*.

The snow monster knew we were there.

Then we saw him. He was standing near my bed. Or rather, he was *crouching* near my bed. He was so huge that he had to bend over to keep from hitting his head on the ceiling!

In the light of my bedroom, he was uglier than I had even imagined! His hair was long and thick and white, and his teeth were long and razor sharp. His eyes glowed bright red, like shiny apples.

And his claws! They were big and nasty looking . . . just like I had drawn them. They looked sharp enough to tear anything to shreds.

"Gosh," John whispered. *"Did you have to make him so mean?"*

I didn't say anything.

Suddenly the Great Garbonzo swept past me! He was holding out the magic wand, pointing it at the snow monster!

When the creature saw this, he turned and reached for the cane, which was leaning on the bed. He let out a weird snarl that echoed through the room.

Oh no! Mom and Dad were sure to hear that and come running!

The Great Garbonzo was almost upon the snow monster. The giant white beast had the cane in his claws, but the magician was too quick. Before the monster could do anything with the cane, the Great Garbonzo had reached out — and touched him with the tip of the wand!

The monster let out a wail and a screech.

He dropped the cane, and the Great Garbonzo leapt forward, picked it up, and dashed back away.

All of a sudden the giant creature began to shake. It was like he was dissolving. And that's what he was doing!

He was disappearing!

It was a slow process, or at least, it seemed slow. It was like he turned into a faint mist and just shimmered away. In the next moment, he was gone!

I looked over at my poster on the wall. The elves and reindeer were there, and the snowman. Then I could see it! The snow monster! He was returning to my poster! His form was faint at first, then he grew darker and darker! It worked! The Great Garbonzo had sent my snow monster back to where he belonged! Now he was just a harmless drawing on a piece of paper.

Boy, was I relieved. John too, and the magician as well.

"You did it!" I cried. "You sent him back to my poster! You saved us!"

The Great Garbonzo beamed. He leaned forward and tipped his hat, nodding.

"Happy to be of service," he said. "Now. I must —"

"Matt!" I heard someone yell from downstairs.

Dad! Oh no! He must have heard the snow monster scream! How would I explain the magician and John in my bedroom?

I dashed quickly out the door and closed it behind me. Dad was coming up the stairs.

"Keep your music down," he said. "You'll drive your mother nuts." He wasn't really mad. It was more like a warning. And with that, he turned and went back down the stairs.

That was a close one!

I went back into my bedroom and closed the door behind me.

"No problem," I said to John and the Great Garbonzo.

The magician handed me the wand.

"I suggest," he began, "that you read the manual that this came with. It will save a lot of trouble."

I took the wand from him.

"Thanks," I said. "I will. Promise."

"And now, I must return to the Secret Mist. I'm a busy magician, you know."

I thanked him for everything, and John did, too.

The Great Garbonzo nodded and tipped his hat again, and, holding his cane out before him, muttered some strange words.

He was vanishing! Right before our eyes, he was fading away, just like the snow monster had done. Soon, he was gone completely.

John and I stared for a moment.

"Wow," he said finally. "Nobody's going to believe this."

"You're right," I said. "It's too wild."

I looked at my alarm clock next to my bed. "You have to get out of here," I said, "before Mom and Dad see you."

John looked at the clock. "Quarter to nine?!?!?" he exclaimed. "I was supposed to be home by now!"

"Come on," I said. "Let's sneak

167

downstairs."

We tip-toed down the stairs. I could hear the TV in the living room, and from where I stood I could see Dad sitting in his chair. He was munching on some popcorn, still watching the news.

So far, so good.

Suddenly we heard footsteps. Mom! Oh no! Mom was coming! She had been in the kitchen and now she was going back to the living room . . . but she would have to come right past us!

"Quick!" I whispered to John. *"Duck behind the foyer door again!"*

John did as I asked . . . just as Mom came around the corner!

"There you are," she said, smiling. She handed me a cookie.

"Thanks, Mom," I said. Chocolate-chip cookies are my favorite.

"So . . . did you see any snow monsters while you were outside?"

Whoops.

"Wh . . . what . . . what do you mean?" I stammered. I was sure I had been caught.

"Oh, Mrs. Berringer just called. She claims that she saw a snow monster. She was so scared, she even called the police!"

"Imagine that," I muttered. It was all I could think to say.

"No, I think *she* imagined that," Mom answered. "Good grief . . . a snow monster! Sometimes I think Mrs. Berringer has an imagination like *yours.*"

"Maybe," I said. Mom turned and walked into the living room.

Whew!

When I was sure that she wasn't coming back, I whispered to John that it was all clear. He slipped out from behind the door.

"I gotta go," he said.

"Thanks, man," I said, and we slapped our hands together in a high-five.

"We did it," he said.

"Yeah, we did," I responded. In my other hand, I still had the chocolate-chip cookie that Mom gave me. I handed it to John. "For the walk home," I said. He popped it in his mouth.

"Thanks," he mumbled, smiling and chewing at the same time.

I opened the door and he quietly went out.

"See ya tomorrow," I called out.

"You bet," he said, then he stopped and turned back toward me. "And Matt?" he said.

"Yeah?"

He finished off the last bite of the cookie and smiled as he spoke.

"Read that manual," he said.

I nodded and frowned. "Don't worry," I said. "Don't worry."

I closed the door.

32

Christmas day was a blast. I got a bunch of
PokeMon cards and a cool model airplane, and
a bunch of other great stuff.

Later that afternoon, my twin cousins
Alex and Adrian showed up. They're great.
Alex is a girl, Adrian is a boy. They're twelve,
and they live in Petoskey, which is about an
hour away. A lot of people came over that day
for a big Christmas dinner.

I hadn't touched my magic kit since the
snow monster incident. I figured that when I

had time to read the manual, I would get it back out again. I did NOT want any more problems!

Needless to say, I didn't put on a magic show for Christmas.

After dinner the adults sat in the living room. Kimmy was playing with her dolls in her room.

"Hey you guys," I said to Alex and Adrian. "Come and see what my Grandma and Grandpa gave me for Christmas."

They followed me to my bedroom and I pulled out the magic kit from beneath my bed.

"It's a real one," I said. "I mean . . . you can really do magic with this kit. Not just tricks."

"Wow," Alex said.

"That's cool!" chimed Adrian. "Let's do some magic!"

"Sorry," I said, shaking my head. "Not until I read the manual."

I told them all about the problems with the snow monster and the elves and the reindeer. I even showed them the poster.

"You mean . . . you brought that snowman

to life?" Alex asked. Her eyes just about bugged out of her head!

"Just like Frankenstein," I said. "Only worse. Anyway, I promised the Great Garbonzo that I wouldn't try any more magic until I read the manual."

"The Great *what?*" Adrian asked.

"That's the magician. He lives in the Secret Mist."

Alex brushed her hair out of her face and picked up the wand.

"Careful," I said.

"We could have really used this last summer," she said. Adrian nodded in agreement.

"Why?" I asked. "What happened?"

Alex looked at Adrian, and he at her, as if they weren't sure if they should say anything.

"Well, I guess we can tell you," Alex said. "We found out that our house in Petoskey was haunted!"

"Haunted?" I asked. I didn't believe in ghosts, but Alex and Adrian weren't making this up.

"That's right," Adrian said, nodding. "Poltergeists."

"Polter . . . *what?*" I asked.

"Poltergeists," Alex explained. "It's another word for 'ghosts'. We found out that they were in our house! Wanna hear about it?"

"Are you kidding?!?! Tell me! This I've *got* to hear!"

Next in the
'Michigan Chillers'
series:
#3 — 'Poltergeists of Petoskey'
Go to the next page for a few
spine-tingling chapters!

"Would you quit trying to scare me? Just go to sleep, will you?"

It was my twin brother, Adrian.

Here it was, the middle of the night, and he was standing at the door of my bedroom, scolding me for doing something—even though I was half asleep!

"What are you talking about?" I asked groggily. I was angry. It was late, and I didn't appreciate being awakened at such an hour. Even if it was summer, and even if I *did* get to sleep in a little.

"You," he hissed. He was mad! "Quit walking by my door and making noises!"

Huh? What was he talking about?

"I'm not walking by your door," I said, yawning.

What would make him think such a thing? I had been sleeping. I'm not going to wake up in the middle of the night just to try and scare him!

"I heard you walk by my door," he continued, wagging a pointed finger in my direction. *"Again.* Just like last night."

It was hard to see him in the dark. He was just a dark shape that was standing in my doorway.

"You're crazy," I chided. "I've been *sleeping!"*

"Yeah, well knock it off or I'm going to tell Mom and Dad."

Fine. Let him tell Mom and Dad. I was telling him the truth . . . I've been sleeping. Besides . . . why would I waste my time trying to scare Adrian in the middle of the night? He's easy enough to scare during the day.

My name is Alexis, but everyone calls me Alex. I'm twelve. My brother Adrian and I are twins. Not identical twins, but fraternal twins. He's a boy, I'm a girl. And, if I do say so myself, I was given a few more brains than my brother. Of course, he disagrees with me, but that just shows how wrong he can be.

I have lived in Petoskey my whole life. It's great here! I mean, since I haven't lived anywhere else, I guess I can't really say if there's anyplace better, but I sure do like Petoskey. It's a small city in northwest Michigan, right next to Lake Michigan. It's beautiful! There are lots of pretty beaches and forests and all kinds of things to do.

My favorite thing to do in the whole world is swim. I love swimming! I swim in pools, in the lake—anyplace where there is water! Adrian doesn't like the water as much as I do, but he likes going to the beach. We don't live very far from the Petoskey State Park, so he and I walk there a lot.

Last year, Mom and Dad started looking for a new house. They said that the one we lived in had become too small, and that we all needed more space. They said that I would get a bigger bedroom!

THAT would be great! I mean . . . I liked the house that we were living in at the time . . . but Mom and Dad were right—it *was* kind of small.

Anyway, when Mom and Dad said that they had found a new house for us, I was really excited—until I saw it.

It was an *old* house!

An old farmhouse, to be exact. It sat in the middle of a field, cold and alone, and it looked like it had been empty for years! When Mom and Dad asked what we thought about it, I told them that I thought it was falling apart. It was true! Shingles had fallen off the roof, and there were holes through the walls. Who on earth could live in a house like that? It was a wreck—and Mom and Dad agreed!

But they said that if it was fixed up right, it would be beautiful once again. I didn't see how then, but *now* I do!

Mom and Dad bought the house and we

spent last summer working on it. There was a lot of work that we had to do. Adrian and I helped with some of it. Mostly, we just hauled all of the old junk out to the big dumpster.

But Mom and Dad were right! After we fixed it up, it sure was beautiful. All of the rooms have hardwood floors and high ceilings. And lots and lots of room! Mom and Dad said that they wanted to make the house look just like it did when it was first built—way back in 1897!

Wow! We were going to live in a house that was over one hundred years old!

There was only one problem, and it was a big one: GHOSTS!

2

Now . . . before you think that I'm really weird or something, let me tell you . . . I had never believed in ghosts before . . . but I sure do now!

Here's what happened:

One night not long after we moved in, I was sleeping in my bedroom. Mom and Dad said I could decorate it any way that I wanted. My bedroom is really neat . . . I have paintings and pictures of horses on the walls. I even have a poster of a horse on my ceiling! I really like horses.

Anyway, I went to bed early, before

anyone else. I was tired! I had been swimming most of the day, and then my friend Stacey and I went horseback riding. Stacey lives a couple miles away. They have a farm and a few horses. Dad says that we might get horses some day. I hope so.

I was tired when I got home, so I went to bed early. It was so early that the sun was still up.

The problem was, when I woke up, it was *dark*. I couldn't get back to sleep. The clock next to my bed said that it was almost four in the morning—but I was wide a wake!

And I was thirsty. So I got up to get a glass of water.

Living in an old home is cool. But it can be spooky sometimes, too. When you walk on the old wood floor, it creaks and moans. Sometimes the house makes noises in the night. It was a bit scary the first couple nights, but I got used to it.

As I walked down the stairs, the steps creaked beneath my feet. Nothing unusual.

But when I got to the bottom of the stairs,

the creaking sound continued!

I just stood there, looking up at the darkened staircase. I could hear the steps squeak, just like someone was walking on them . . . but there was no one there! I was terrified, but I was too afraid to even move.

Suddenly the squeaking stopped. The house got really quiet. Still, I was too afraid to move. I don't know how long I stood there in my nightgown, frozen to the floor, watching. Shadows loomed out at me, and I imagined that they were like dark animals, waiting to attack.

After some time, I got up the courage to walk to the kitchen. In our kitchen we have a small stove light that stays on all the time. It gives off enough light to see pretty good in the dark.

I got a glass of water and gulped it down. When I sat it back on the counter, I noticed something strange.

All of the cupboard doors in the kitchen had opened! Not just a little bit, but all the way open! I knew that they were closed when I first walked into the kitchen.

So . . . I closed all of them. There were twelve cupboard doors that had opened. I stood there for a moment, looking at them, wondering if they would open up again.

They didn't.

Whew. That was too freaky.

I left the kitchen and went back to bed. I was a little nervous going back up the stairs, thinking that I might hear the strange creaking on the steps again. I didn't, and I was glad. I crawled back into bed and finally was able to fall asleep.

When I awoke in the morning, the sun was already up. Birds were singing in the yard, and I heard an airplane buzzing high in the sky. I threw on my sweats and an old T-shirt, and went downstairs. Mom was in the kitchen.

"Hi Sweets," she said, kissing me on the cheek as I sat down on a stool. Mom has called me 'Sweets' for as long as I can remember.

"Good morning," I yawned. "Is there any juice left?"

Mom reached into the fridge and pulled out a pitcher. There was just enough orange juice left to fill a glass.

"Finish that up and I'll make some more. Your father and your brother will be up soon, and they'll want some."

She poured a glass and I sipped it. It was cold and sweet and tangy.

"Oh," she said, opening the freezer. She pulled out a can of frozen orange juice and ran it under hot water in the sink. "Did you get up and come downstairs last night?" she asked.

"Mm-hmm," I muttered, sipping on the glass of orange juice and nodding my head.

"I thought so. What on earth were you looking for?"

"What do you mean?" I asked, putting the empty glass down on the counter.

"The cupboard doors, of course. *All of them were open when I got up this morning.*"

3

Later that day, I told my brother about the cupboards.

"That's really weird," he said.

I couldn't figure out how those cupboard doors opened. It was like they opened all by themselves! I thought that maybe I just *dreamed* that I closed them when I got up to get a glass of water. At least, that's what I tried to tell myself.

But I wasn't really scared. I was sure that there had to be some reason. What that reason was, I didn't know.

Nothing happened the next night or the

night after that. Actually, a few nights went by before something else happened. Something that scared the daylights out of me!

I had almost forgotten about the cupboard incident. Late one night I got up again to get a glass of water. I was sleepy and the house was dark. No one else was awake.

But when I got to the kitchen, there was already a glass of water poured! It even had ice in it. It sat right on the counter in plain view.

Freaky!

I didn't know if I should drink it or not. But no one else was awake. How a glass of ice water was poured in the middle of the night was a mystery.

So I drank it. It was icy-cold and good. I kept expecting Mom or Dad or Adrian to come into the room and ask me why I drank their water, but they never did.

After I finished it, I poured the ice into the sink. It was still very late (or early, depending on how you looked at it) and I wanted to hop back into my warm bed.

I reached for the glass to place it in the

dishwasher. Mom's real strict about that. If we use a dish or a glass, rinse it off and put it in the dishwasher, pronto. I reached for the glass.

It was full!

The glass sat on the counter, *filled with water and ice!*

Had I done it and forgot about it?

No, I hadn't. I was sure.

I looked in the sink. The ice was still there from when I had emptied the glass.

That freaked me out. I didn't even stay long enough to empty the glass and put it in the dishwasher. I'd explain to Mom in the morning. Right now I just wanted to curl up in bed and pull the sheets over my head!

I left the kitchen and tip-toed up the stairs. The steps cried out and protested beneath my bare feet. Then I remembered the other night, when the steps had continued to creak, even when there was no one there. When I reached the top of the stairs I stopped, expecting the stairs to keep squeaking. They didn't, and I was glad.

My bedroom door was open, and bright

moonlight lit up the floor. My window was open and the night air was warm and fresh. I could hear thousands of crickets chiming in the field. It was the only sound I heard, and I had grown attached to the gentle whirring of the insects. The sound of crickets meant that it was time for sleep.

I felt better, I guess, hearing the crickets, and my fear left me. There had to be some explanation about the glass, I told myself. There *had* to be. Maybe Mom or Dad had left the glass out before they went to bed. Maybe they even left it for me. I would ask them in the morning. That didn't explain how the glass got re-filled, but there had to be some logical reason for that, too.

There *had* to be.

I stood for a moment looking out the open window. The field was glowing in the moonlight. It was beautiful.

When I turned to crawl back into bed, I caught my reflection in the mirror, and what I saw made me cold with fright.

There was someone else in the mirror! I

could see the dark reflection of someone — or something — standing behind me!

4

"Ohhh!" I screamed.

Actually, I didn't really scream. I think I was too afraid! It sounded more like a loud drawing in of breath. Both of my hands flew up, covering my open mouth.

I spun.

It was Adrian!

I should have known! He was standing in my doorway in his pajamas.

"Geez," he snickered. "You sure get spooked easy!"

"That was *not* funny!" I scolded. And it

wasn't.

"I wasn't trying to scare you," he said. "I heard a noise and I got up to see what it was. It was just you."

"I got up to get a glass of water," I explained coldly. "Is that illegal in my own home?" I was still shaking from the scare, and I was angry.

Then he did something that I couldn't believe! He apologized! Adrian *actually* apologized!

"Gosh, I'm sorry about that, Al," he said. "I really didn't mean to."

"That's okay," I said. "It's just that . . . well, there's a couple weird things that have been going on."

"Like the glass of water?" he asked.

He knew!

"How did you—was that *you*? Did you put the glass of water there?"

He shook his head from side to side. "Not me, Alex," he said. "But I've seen it a couple times. I go to get a glass of water, and it's already waiting. Then, after I drink it—"

" — it fills itself back up again," I said. He nodded in agreement. "And I suppose you've seen the cupboards too, huh?"

"Yes," I whispered. "They open and close by themselves."

Adrian shifted in the doorway.

"Gosh Al," he said quietly. "Do you think the house is . . . *haunted?* Do think that we live in a haunted house?"

"No way," I said. "There's no such thing as ghosts."

"But how do we explain the water glass filling up all by itself? And the cupboards opening by themselves? Something really weird is going on in this house, Alex. *Really* weird."

A chill snaked along my spine like a tiny mouse scurrying up and down my back. It was the way Adrian had said those two words:

Really weird.

He was right. There was something really weird going on, that was for sure.

But what?

"Remember a few nights ago?" he asked me. "Remember when I came to your bedroom and told you to stop trying to scare me?"

I nodded.

"Well, I heard something that night. Like footsteps. Up and down the stairs and across the hall. It was just like someone was walking on the floor, only no one was there. That's why I thought you did it."

"It wasn't me," I whispered.

"I know that now . . . because now I hear the footsteps almost every night."

I shuddered. "I've heard them too," I said. "A couple of nights ago when I went down to the kitchen. When I got to the bottom of the stairs, the steps kept squeaking like there was someone walking on them."

We were silent for a moment, listening to the chorus of crickets drifting through the open window. The drapes fluttered softly in the gentle breeze, and the field was aglow by the light of the moon.

"What do we do?" I asked.

"Beats me," Adrian replied. "But it sure is freaking me out. I wish it would stop."

"Maybe if we asked it to go away, it

would," I offered.

"*What* would?" Adrian wondered aloud. "We don't even know what—or who—this is. We don't—"

"*Sssshhh!*" I whispered, placing a finger to my lips. "*I just heard something!*"

He stopped talking, and we listened.

Nothing. Just crickets.

Listening . . . .

"What did you hear?" Adrian whispered, leaning toward me so he wouldn't have to raise his voice any higher than he needed. "I don't—"

But he stopped short of his sentence.

Creeeaaakkkkk . . . kkkk . . . eeaakkkkk.

Adrian's eyes grew to the size of golf balls! I guess mine probably did, too.

Creaak . . . Creeeeeeeeee . . . eeeek . . . .

It was louder. Whatever it was, it was coming closer. It was coming up the steps!

About the author

Johnathan Rand is the author of the best-selling **'Chillers'** series, <u>now with over 1,000,000 copies in print.</u> In addition to the **'Chillers'** series, Rand is also the author of **'Ghost in the Graveyard',** a collection of thrilling, original short stories featuring *The Adventure Club.* (And don't forget to check out **www.ghostinthegraveyard.com** and read an **entire story** from 'Ghost in the Graveyard' *FREE!*) When Mr. Rand and his wife are not traveling to schools and book signings, they live in a small town in northern lower Michigan with their two dogs, Abby and Salty. He still writes all of his books in the wee hours of the morning, and still submits all manuscripts by mail. He is currently working on his newest series, entitled **'American Chillers'.** His popular website features hundreds of photographs, stories, and art work. Visit:

www.americanchillers.com

Terror Stalks Traverse City Word Search!

```
R E T S O P H T R Y V L K V O F J X H X
S Z A E L K W R L X D J U P V U L R G J
L W S C A P E U E T E E R T S T N O R F
R W T R A V E R S E C I T Y K R B Z N H
C N D E E L K L T D J G E E F E M N J R
U Y F T X L E N A C O S N L Z T K O P Z
M C E M Y U L E H U H T A V R S H B Q N
N G Z I Q J O I K X N R V E U N Z R G B
X F V S R P A N H A Z A E S A O Z A Y V
A E E T N L S E M C Z D M T L M H G W K
D C V Y X D Y W I H N A H L M W P T V O
O C N X Q L O K S I Z A A A D O M A P N
I L E A V N T V E T N L G M Z N H E S G
I B L D S K R R A N O I F I L S N R G J
I H R O K Q X E R Z C O X S H S P G K B
A C I P F X S A C K Y Q U Q P C A T T D
U F E Q O B N H I Q P U T A M Z I S L A
Z U G X A D B T J A V W C X H U Y M X I
J L L J H V S O C L D E V J F S A Q D V
A K A X P Q N Q A K M Y B I Z Q J M F Z
```

aleekazaam	manual
cane	Matt
cape	Secret Mist
Michigan Chillers	snow monster
Traverse City	Open Space
elves	poster
Front Street	reindeer
Great Garbonzo	snowman
hat	magic kit
John	Johnathan Rand

Word Scramble!

Unscramble the words and place the new words in the blanks!

etvrresa ytci   _ _ _ _ _ _ _ _   _ _ _ _

bozagnro   _ _ _ _ _ _ _ _

eonp aescp   _ _ _ _   _ _ _ _ _

lsvee   _ _ _ _ _

ihngcmai seclihrl   _ _ _ _ _ _ _ _   _ _ _ _ _ _ _ _

cetsre stmi   _ _ _ _ _ _   _ _ _ _

wosn trenoms   _ _ _ _   _ _ _ _ _ _ _

rorert   _ _ _ _ _ _

igcma nadw   _ _ _ _ _   _ _ _ _

erdrneie   _ _ _ _ _ _ _ _

rmscishta   _ _ _ _ _ _ _ _

About the cover art: This unique cover was designed and created by Darrin Brege and Mark Thompson.

Darrin Brege works as an animator by day, and is now applying his talents on the internet, creating various web sites and flash animations. He attended animation school in southern California in the early nineties, and over the years has created original characters and animations for Warner Bros (Space Jam), for Hasbro (Tonka Joe Multimedia line), Universal Pictures (Bullwinkle and Fractured Fairy Tales CD Roms), and Disney. Besides art, he and his wife Karen are improv performers featured weekly at Mark Ridley's Comedy Castle over the last six years. Improvisational comedy has provided the groundwork for a successful voice over career as well. Darrin has dozens of characters and impersonations in his portfolio and, most recently, provided Columbia Tri-Star pictures with a Nathan Lane 'sound alike' for Stuart Little. Speaking of little, Darrin and Karen also have a little son named Mick.

Mark Thompson has been in the illustration field for over 20 years, working for everyone from the Detroit Tigers, Ameritech, as well as auto companies and toy companies such as Hasbro and Mattel. Mark's main interests are in science fiction and fantasy art. He works from his studio in a log home in the woods of Hamburg Michigan. Mark is married with 2 children, and says he is also a big-time horror fan and comic collector!

also available from Johnathan Rand:

All AudioCraft books are proudly printed, bound, and manufactured in the United States of America, utilizing American resources, labor, and materials.

USA